# Lauren Child

# Absolutely ONE Thing

## Featuring Charlie and Lola

CANDLEWICK PRESS

4 2sday For Tuesday

1

Copyright © 2015 by Lauren Child. Text design © 2015 by David Mackintosh.

First U.S. paperback edition 2018

First published in Great Britain in 2015 by Orchard Books

Library of Congress Catalog Card Number 2015933254

ISBN 978-0-7636-8728-1 (hardcover)

ISBN 978-1-5362-0038-6 (paperback)

22 23 APS 10 9 8 7 6 5 4 3

Printed in Humen, Dongguan, China

This book was typeset in ITC Officina Serif.

Candlewick Press
99 Dover Street
Somerville,
Massachusetts 02144

visit us at www.candlewick.com

I have this little sister, Lola.
She is small and very funny.

Sometimes for a treat,
Mom says, "We are going to
the store and you may choose
one thing."

"One thing EACH," I say,
        "or ONE thing
                **between** TWO?"

And Mom says, "EACH."

I say to Lola,
"We are going to the store and we are allowed to choose ONE thing."

"One thing to **share?**"
                    says Lola.

I say,
"One thing EACH,
which means TWO actual things."

            "**Two things?**" says Lola.

        "TWO things **between** TWO," I say.

Mom says we must be ready in TEN minutes.

It takes me THREE minutes to brush my teeth,

ONE minute to remember that I have forgotten to eat breakfast,

FOUR minutes to eat my puffa pops,

THREE
minutes
to brush my teeth again

and
EIGHT
minutes
to find Lola's

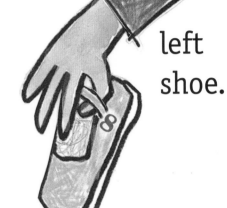

left
shoe.

$$3+1+4+3+8=19$$

That makes us

NINE
MINUTES
LATE.

$$19-10=$$

**9** MINUTES LATE.

Lola shouts,
"I just need to do **SOMething**."

I say,
"WHAT thing?"

She says,
"**One** thing."

I say,
"But we don't
have time…"

She says,
"I will be **half** of
a **second**."

This is NOT TRUE because after TWO whole minutes, which is in fact 120 SECONDS, I go into our room to find Lola.

"What are you DOING?" I say.

Lola says,
"I am just trying to count the dots on my dress.
But I am
NOT sure what
comes after
twelve."

I say, "Missing going to the store comes after twelve."

"Oh," says Lola. "HURRY Up!"

I am running as fast as I can and Lola is counting ladybugs on the path.

She says,

"There are at least FIFTY or twenty-seventeen.

How many shoes would FIFTY or twenty-SEVENTEEN ladybugs need, Charlie?"

I say, "NONE, ladybugs DON'T WEAR SHOES."

"What about SOCKS?" says Lola.

"No, they NEVER wear socks."

"It must be very ouchy," says Lola.

When we walk past the pond
we are followed by several ducks.

"How many ducks are following us?" asks Lola.

"THREE," I say.

Lola finds half a cookie in her coat pocket and starts feeding them crumbs.

"How many **now**?" she says.

I say, "**THREE** ducks, **SEVEN** pigeons, **FIVE** wading birds, **FOUR** swans, **TWO** geese, and **ONE** flapping bird."

$3+7+5+4+2+1=22$

"Run!"

shouts Lola.

Lola looks up at the sky and she says,
"Look at all of **those** singing birds — there are

one two five SEVEN twenty
sixteen eleventen NINE birds singing."

1 2

are

there

And I say, "NO, Lola,

I say,
"Well, if you are
so good at counting,
then how many **leaves**
are there on that tree?"

"A **hundred**," says Lola,
"nearly at **least**."

I say,
"There are
MORE THAN
a **hundred**,
more than
A THOUSAND,
even."

"How many is a **thousand**?" says Lola.

"TEN HUNDREDS make A THOUSAND," I say.

$$10 \times 100 = 1000$$

"And is a **thousand** the **most**?" says Lola.

I say, "No, then there is a MILLION and that is

"And is a **million** MORE than the **rain**?" says Lola

"or **maybe** even a TRILLION."

"Or a **squil**

a **THOUSAND** times **more**."

"No, the rain is probably a **billion**," I say,

**ion?"** says Lola.

I say,
"I don't know if a
SQUILLION is a **number**."

When we get there, Mom says, "You may choose one thing."

And Lola says, "**Three** things."

teps to walk to the store.

**156**

1
2

And Mom says,
"ONE thing."

**1**

And Lola says,
"**Two** things."

**2**

And Mom says,
"How about NO things?"

And Lola says,
"How
about
**one**
thing?"

And Mom says,
"Absolutely ONE thing."

And Lola says,

"Yes, **one** thing."

I spend THREE minutes looking at the comics
and TWO minutes looking at the pins and
I make up my mind in FIVE seconds.

I choose the
SIX pins.

Lola is still looking.

After **ELEVEN** minutes, Mom says,
"Hurry up, Lola, we are leaving in
one minute."

**TWO** minutes
later, Lola
chooses **twelve**
stickers.

On the way home, Lola sticks FIVE stickers on the pavement, THREE on a tree, TWO on her shoes, and ONE on me. She even sticks ONE on Marv's dog.

By the time we get home there are NO stickers left.

NONE.

12 - 5 - 3 - 2 - 1 - 1 = 0

Sadlier

# CHRIST IN US™

## Parish Edition 4

*Shammah Folefac*

*Shammah Folefac*

*"Christ In Us Grade 4 cover artwork speaks to the students' discovery of their role as 'sowers of the seed' of faith in their Church and community."*

Reverend Donald Senior, C.P., S.T.D.

**S Sadlier Religion**

This advanced publication copy has been printed prior to final publication and pending ecclesiastical approval.

## Acknowledgments

This publication was printed with permission pending from the following copyright holders.

Excerpts from the *Catechism of the Catholic Church, second edition*, © 2000, Libreria Editrice Vaticana—United States Conference of Catholic Bishops, Washington, D. C. All rights reserved.

Scripture texts in this work are taken from the *New American Bible, revised edition* © 2010, 1991, 1986, 1970 Confraternity of Christian Doctrine, Washington, D. C. All Rights Reserved. No part of the New American Bible may be reproduced in any form without permission in writing from the copyright owner.

Excerpts from the English translation of *The Roman Missal* © 2010 International Commission on English in the Liturgy, Inc. (ICEL). All rights reserved.

Quotations from papal addresses, audiences, homilies, speeches, messages, meditations, encyclicals, and other Vatican documents are from www.vatican.va and copyright © by Libreria Editrice Vaticana.

Excerpts from *The Order of Confirmation*. Copyright © 2016 ICEL. All rights reserved.

Excerpts from *Rite of Baptism for Children*. Copyright © 1969, ICEL. All rights reserved.

Excerpts from *The Order of Celebrating Matrimony*. Copyright © 2016 ICEL. All rights reserved.

Excerpts from the Web sites of the Order of Carmelites, Catholic News Service, and the Mystical Humanity of Christ © 2019. All rights reserved.

Excerpts from "O Come, O Come, Emanuel" GIA music. © 1996 by GIA Publications, Inc., 7404 S. Mason Ave., Chicago, IL 60638 • www.giamusic.com • 800.442.1358. All rights reserved.

Excerpts from "Go Tell It on the Mountain" GIA music. © 2005 by GIA Publications, Inc., 7404 S. Mason Ave., Chicago, IL 60638 • www.giamusic.com • 800.442.1358. All rights reserved.

Excerpts from "The Eyes and Hands of Christ" © 2019 Tom Kendzia. Published by OCP 5536 NE Hassalo St., Portland, OR 97213. All rights reserved.

Excerpts from "You Have Anointed Me" © 2019 Mike Balhoff; Gary Daigle; Darryl Ducote. Published by OCP 5536 NE Hassalo St., Portland, OR 97213. All rights reserved.

William H. Sadlier, Inc.
9 Pine Street
New York, NY 10005-4700

ISBN: 978-0-8215-3694-0

1 2 3 4 5 6 7 8 9 WEBC 23 22 21 20

*Christ In Us* was developed in collaboration with the wisdom of the community. The team included respected catechetical, liturgical, pastoral, and theological experts who shared their insights and inspired its development.

With grateful acknowledgment of
William Sadlier Dinger and Frank Sadlier Dinger
for their leadership, vision, and commitment to excellence in the development
of Sadlier's catechetical programs and resources since 1963

## Theological and Liturgical Consultants

Most Reverend Christopher James Coyne
Bishop of Burlington, VT

Donna Eschenauer, Ph.D.
Associate Dean, Associate Professor of
 Pastoral Theology
St. Joseph's Seminary and College

Rita Ferrone, M.Div.

Thomas Kendzia
Sadlier National Consultant for
 Liturgy and Music

Reverend Monsignor John Pollard, M. Ed., S.T.L.

Alissa Thorell, M.T.S

John B. Angotti, M.A.P.S.

Barbara Sutton, D.Min.

Kathleen Dorsey Bellow, D.Min.

## Scripture Consultant

Reverend Donald Senior, C.P., S.T.D.
Chancellor and President Emeritus
 Catholic Theological Union

## Catechetical Consultants

Amy Welborn, M.A.

Susan Stark

Sr. Theresa Engel, O.S.F.
Member of the School Sisters of St. Francis

Maureen A. Kelly, M.A.

Karla Manternach, M.A.

Woodeene Koenig-Bricker, M.A.

Connie Clark

Shannon Chisholm, Ph.D.

Susan M. Sink

Maureen Shaughnessy, S.C.

Lori Dahlhoff, Ed.D.

Andrea D. Chavez-Kopp, M.Ed.

## Educational Consultants

Richard Culatta

Heidi Hayes Jacobs, Ed.D.

Jay McTighe

Allie Johnston

## Learning Style Inclusion Consultants

Charleen Katra, M.A.

Jennifer Ochoa, M.Ed., LDT/C

## Inculturation Consultants

Luis J. Medina
Director, Bilingual Catechesis

Charlene Howard, M.A.

Michael P. Howard, M.A.
Eat the Scroll Ministry

## Catholic Social Teaching

Kristin Witte, D.Min.

Genevieve Jordan Laskey, M.A.

Michael Jordan Laskey, M.A.

# Contents

*(prayer symbol)* **Prayer: Praise**

**Psalm 104:24**

• God wants us to know him. • God inspired the writers of Sacred Scripture. • Jesus is the promised Savior. • The Church teaches and guides us.

**Lesson Test:** Show What You Know

**Partners in Faith:** Saint Teresa of Ávila

**Mini-Task:** How can I invite others to share God's love?

**At Home:** Discuss how your family has passed on the Good News.

*(prayer symbol)* **Prayer: Adoration**

**Deuteronomy 7:9**

• God has a loving plan for us. • God reveals himself as Father, Son, and Holy Spirit. • Jesus Christ is the Son of God, our Lord and Savior. • The Holy Spirit guides the Church and makes her holy.

**Lesson Test:** Show What You Know

**Partners in Faith:** Saint Elizabeth of the Trinity

**Mini-Task:** What is God's plan for me?

**At Home:** The Holy Spirit helps and guides us.

*(prayer symbol)* **Prayer: Thanksgiving**

**2 Corinthians 5:7**

• God created us in his image and likeness. • Faith helps us respond to God's love. • Grace helps us live in friendship with the Blessed Trinity. • We are called to live as Jesus' faithful disciples.

**Lesson Test:** Show What You Know

**Partners in Faith:** Saints Louis and Zélie Martin

**Mini-Task:** How can I build my friendship with God and others?

**At Home:** Families help one another choose good.

*(prayer symbol)* **Prayer:** *Lectio* and *Visio Divina*

**Eucharistic Prayer 2,** *Roman Missal*

• Mary was born without Original Sin. • Jesus teaches us how to live. • Because of Jesus' Death and Resurrection, we can have eternal life. • Jesus will come again at the end of time.

*(audio symbol)* **Hail, Mary**

**Lesson Test:** Show What You Know

**Partners in Faith:** Saint Timothy

**Mini-Task:** How does Jesus Christ show me how to live?

**At Home:** As a family we help each other when we feel sad or alone.

*(prayer symbol)* **Prayer: Blessing**

**Matthew 5:16**

• The Church is the Body of Christ. • We are called to share the Good News of Jesus. • The Holy Spirit helps us carry on the mission of the Church. • The pope and bishops serve the Church.

**Lesson Test:** Show What You Know

**Partners in Faith:** Saint Kateri Tekakwitha

**Mini-Task:** How do I share in the mission of the Church?

**At Home:** Renew baptismal promises as a family.

**Lesson Test:** Show What You Know

**Partners in Faith:** Saint Vincent de Paul

**Mini-Task:** How does prayer lead to happiness?

**At Home:** God loves your family just as you are.

**Prayer: Traditional**

**Luke 6:27–28**

• Our prayers praise God and trust in his goodness. • We can pray at all times. • The Mass is the Church's greatest prayer. • We can pray aloud or silently in our hearts.

**Lesson Test:** Show What You Know

**Partners in Faith:** Saint Elizabeth of Portugal

**Mini-Task:** How do I pray for others?

**At Home:** We draw closer to God through different ways of prayer.

**Prayer: Praise**

**1 John 5:14**

• The Church is strengthened and guided by holy men and women. • The virtues of faith, hope, and charity are sources of prayer. • Prayer strengthens Christian family life. • Prayer turns our hearts toward God.

**Lesson Test:** Show What You Know

**Partners in Faith:** Saint Frances of Rome

**Mini-Task:** What helps me to pray?

**At Home:** The quieter we are, the better we can listen to God.

**Prayer: Traditional**

**Matthew 6:8**

• Jesus himself taught us the Lord's prayer. • The Lord's Prayer helps us know God. • In the Lord's Prayer we honor and praise God. • The Lord's Prayer helps us place our trust in God.

**Lesson Test:** Show What You Know

**Partners in Faith:** Blessed Jerzy Popiełuszko

**Mini-Task:** What are some ways I pray with others?

**At Home:** Pray the Our Father with your family in a special way.

# Your Spiritual Journey

*Christ In Us* offers a saint for every grade. As you journey through each unit, remember to pray to your grade's saint. Ask him or her to help guide you to be closer to Jesus Christ.

Saint Teresa was born in Ávila, Spain. As a girl, she loved to read stories about the saints and martyrs. As a teenager, however, Teresa cared more about clothes and how she looked than about God.

After she was sick for a long time, Teresa changed her thinking and decided to become a nun. She taught herself how to pray quietly, in union with God. She became a Carmelite nun and wanted to devote her life to simple, quiet prayer, called contemplative prayer.

Teresa founded many convents and taught other nuns about prayer. She saw many visions of Jesus. Others did not always believe her and made fun of her, but she obeyed God anyway. Several priests came to understand that what happened to Teresa was true.

She wrote about her visions and way of prayer in several books. For her brilliant writings and teachings on prayer, Saint Teresa of Ávila was declared a Doctor of the Church. She is one of only four women saints with this honor.

When today can you find some quiet time to pray?

Welcome to **Christ In Us**, an exciting way to grow in your Catholic faith!

Each one of us is on a journey to love and know Jesus Christ. Imagine if every person who met you knew you were a friend of Christ!

Together in this program

we will **ENCOUNTER** Jesus Christ

we will **ACCOMPANY** him in our lives

we will **WITNESS** to our faith.

You will use this book as well as your online digital portal as you discover and grow closer to Jesus Christ.

As you journey in your faith, you can think about these questions:

*For we are his handiwork, created in Christ Jesus for the good works that God has prepared in advance, that we should live in them.*

*Ephesians 2:10*

Why is it important to have Christ live in you?

What would happen if you did not have Jesus in your life?

How does your faith, the Church, and your family help bring you closer to God?

Every lesson has four Spiraling Main Ideas. Here is an example.

Each lesson has one or more **Faith Words** to help you understand the language of our Catholic faith.

The Holy Spirit fills our hearts with sanctifying grace.

We receive a special kind of grace in the Sacrament of Baptism called **sanctifying grace**. This grace
• allows us to share in God's life
• is strengthened by the sacraments
• is strengthened by actual grace
• leads us to eternal life.

Sanctifying grace allows us to share in God's life. Through the forgiveness of sins, sanctifying grace is restored through the Sacrament of Penance and Reconciliation. Sanctifying grace is not something we can see, touch, or hear. Yet it is more effective than anything because it is from the Holy Spirit.

**Faith Word**

sanctifying grace
see p. 259

Be sure to look at all the wonderful photos and beautiful art found in the pages of your book.

**A**ctivity

God wants us to lead a life of holiness. Using the letters of the word, write an acrostic poem about the things you think of when you hear the word *holy*. Draw a star next to the one word that means the most to you right now.

H _____

O _____

L _____

Y _____

ACCOMPANY   139

As you explore this question, you might be asked to stop and think more about it and then do a short **Activity** to answer it better.

You will be asked to **Show What You Know** by writing the answers to some short questions pertaining to the lesson.

12

You will not be alone as you journey through **Christ In Us**. You will have lots of **Partners in Faith**—saints and other holy people who lived amazing lives—walking with you.

Along with **Saint Teresa of Ávila**, here are some other Partners in Faith whom you will meet throughout the book!

Saints Louis and Zélie Martin

Saint Kateri Tekakwitha

Saint John Paul II

Saint Josephine Bakhita

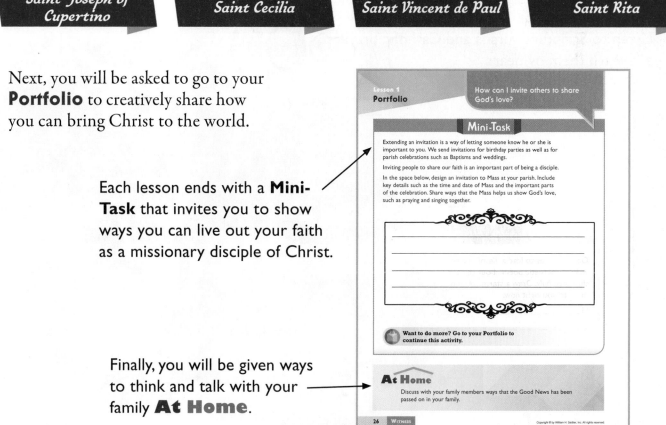

Saint Joseph of Cupertino

Saint Cecilia

Saint Vincent de Paul

Saint Rita

Next, you will be asked to go to your **Portfolio** to creatively share how you can bring Christ to the world.

Each lesson ends with a **Mini-Task** that invites you to show ways you can live out your faith as a missionary disciple of Christ.

Finally, you will be given ways to think and talk with your family **At Home**.

*Christic In Us* features an online portal filled with exciting media and activities to go with the lessons in your book. If you see one of these icons below in your book, you know it's time to visit the student portal for more. (Note: Not every icon will appear in your book.)

Participate in lesson prayers, whose words are online and downloadable

Learn more about the lesson's **Did You Know?** topic by watching an interesting video and doing an activity

Learn more about the lesson's **Partner in Faith** by watching an online video and completing the activity that follows

Listen to Scripture verses and Catholic prayers and learn them by heart

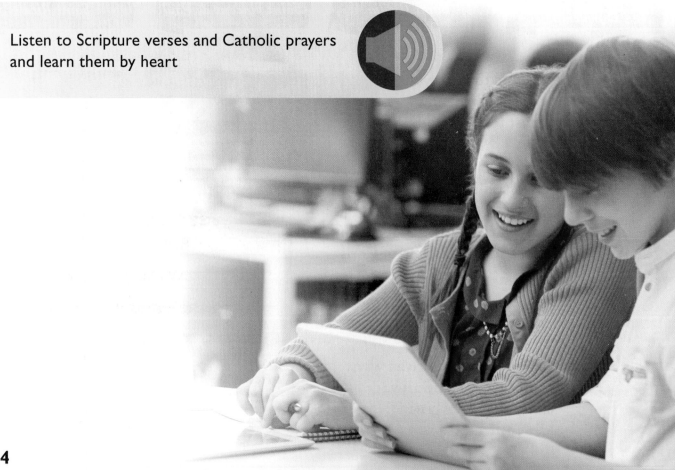

Find fun activities to share and recall what you have learned

**Show What You Know** by completing online assessments

 Read and remember the **Faith Words** definitions

Complete projects and tasks in the online **Portfolio** or *Portfolio Workbook*

 Listen to the songs for your grade level and sing along!

## Your Songs for Grade 4

| Unit Songs | Liturgical Catechesis Seasonal Songs |
|---|---|
| **Unit 1:** "We Have Been Told," David Haas | **Advent:** "Christ, Circle Round Us," Dan Schutte |
| **Unit 2:** "Light of Christ," Tom Kendzia | **Christmas:** "Joy to the World," public domain |
| **Unit 3:** "I Send You Out," John Angotti | **Easter:** "Sing to the Mountains," Bob Dufford, SJ |
| **Unit 4:** "Here I Am, Lord," Dan Schutte | **Pentecost:** "Lord, Send Out Your Spirit," Craig Colson |
| **Unit 5:** "We Are Called," David Haas | |

## Your journey continues with your login to *Christ In Us* Digital!

Here you can explore all the exciting resources that blend together with your textbook.

Take a look at your personalized online dashboard. Everything you need is at your fingertips!

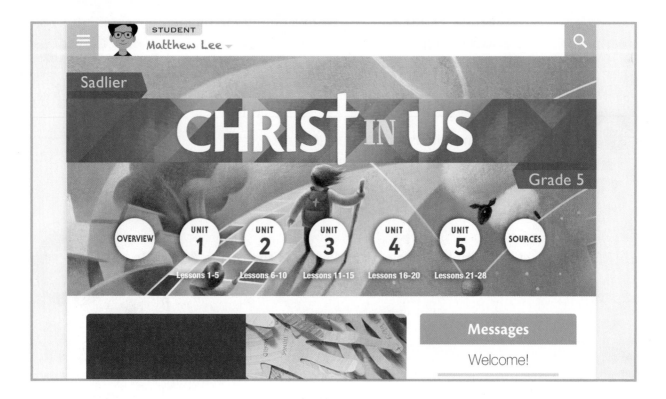

- Think of your portfolio as your digital backpack! Here you can get your assignments, see reminders, send emails, and even talk to your catechist.

- Interactive Mini-Tasks are where you will be able to share exciting activities with others. You will be able to get hands on and creative by making videos or interactive posters.

- Listen with your heart and pray the prayers of *Lectio* and *Visio Divina*, praise, petition, intercession, litany, meditation, blessing, and thanksgiving from your lesson.

- Track your progress with digital quizzes and tests.

## Have a wonderful year!

What do we believe?

The Annunciation

# Unit Prayer

**Leader:** Saint Teresa of Ávila believed it is important for us to leave a place for God in our hearts. She knew how much God loved her, and she spent much of her life seeking a place for God in her own heart.

Let us listen to how the missionary disciples among us live a life filled with God's presence.

**Leader:** Let us pray: Dear God, help us to make room in our hearts for you in our daily lives. If we are to live as Jesus taught us, we need to listen with open hearts and minds. It is for your presence in our lives that we pray:

**Reader:** That we grow more deeply in love with God in our mind,

**All:** fill us with your presence, O God.

**Reader:** That we grow more deeply in love with God in our bodies,

**All:** fill us with your presence, O God.

**Reader:** That we grow more deeply in love with God in our hearts,

**All:** fill us with your presence, O God.

**Reader:** That you fill our souls with your peace and love,

**All:** fill us with your presence, O God.

*End the Unit Prayer by singing the song for this unit.*

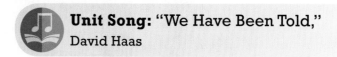

**Unit Song:** "We Have Been Told," David Haas

## Missionary Discipleship

When was a time that you allowed God to be more present to you? When do you make time for yourself to let God's Word speak to you? Can you think of something that you remember that God has given to you? How did you feel?

# How do we know God?

We know God by his love for us. At every moment, and in every corner of the world, God shows us his love. We see it in his amazing work of creation. We read about his love in the Bible. We can see his love most fully and clearly in his Son, Jesus. We also see God's love in his Church. Wherever we look, we will always find our loving God.

**Go to the digital portal for a prayer of praise.**

*"How varied are your works, Lord!*
*In wisdom you have made them all;*
*the earth is full of your creatures."*

Psalm 104:24

## God wants us to know him.

God invites you to get to know him. All the things you've seen today—sky, trees, animals, water, people—are things that God has created and gifts that God gives to draw you closer to him.

We cannot see or hear God the same way we see or hear people. God is a mystery. That means we cannot fully understand or explain his existence and infinite love on our own. So God reveals his love in ways we can understand. We call this **Divine Revelation**. To reveal something means to make it known to others.

Divine Revelation is an invitation to get to know God. The Bible tells us about God sharing his love and goodness with the first humans, Adam and Eve. He made promises to Noah and

**Faith Word**

**Divine Revelation** see p. 257

Abraham. He gave laws to Moses to help people to live in his friendship. Even when times were hard, God spoke through prophets such as Isaiah, who invited people to trust in God.

The greatest revelation of God's love is his Son, Jesus Christ. In Jesus, we find everything we need to know about who God is, because Jesus is both true God and true man. Jesus wants us to share his Father's invitation to love. Through the Holy Spirit, Jesus has given us the Church, so that we can live in God's love and friendship forever.

How would I invite someone to get to know me?

# Did You Know?

**God speaks to us through the Bible.**

## God inspired the writers of Sacred Scripture.

Events in the lives of Noah, Abraham, Moses, and early Church Fathers were shared through many generations of God's people. They were written down and collected in the Bible, which we also call **Sacred Scripture**. The word *scripture* means "holy writing."

The Holy Spirit inspired and guided the people who wrote Sacred Scripture. This means they were able to write without error what God wanted them to write. But they also had the freedom to write in their own way. This is why we say that human beings wrote the Bible, but God is the true author of the Bible.

The Bible is made up of two main sections. The Old Testament tells the story of Creation and the loving promises that God made with his people. The New Testament tells us how

God's promises are kept and fulfilled in our Savior, Jesus Christ. In the New Testament, we learn about Jesus' life and mission. We read about how the early Church spread Jesus' message about his Father's love.

The Holy Spirit helps us to recognize that the basic meaning of Sacred Scripture is a message of salvation and hope. When we read all the history, prophecy, poetry, parables, prayers, sayings, and letters in the Bible, we begin to see that God has a plan for us: to believe in him, love him, trust him, and live in joy with him forever. We see how God means for us to share his love with all people.

### Faith Word

**Sacred Scripture** see p. 259

---

## What Makes Us Catholic?

Knowing the Bible is an important part of being Catholic. Each Sunday at Mass, we hear readings from the Old Testament, the New Testament, and the Gospels, as well as the Psalms.

---

## Activity

The Bible has two main parts: the Old Testament and the New Testament. Make a list of some events you have learned about from each part and look them up in the Bible.

| Event | Old Testament | New Testament |
|---|---|---|
|  |  |  |
|  |  |  |

Tell a partner or a friend about the event you picked.
What can you learn from it?

**Jesus is the promised Savior.**

In the Old Testament, we read about God and his friendship with his people. We see that God never stopped loving them, even when they turned away from him. God made covenants with them—special, solemn promises to care for his people forever. His most important promise was to send his own Son, Jesus, our Savior, who would truly show God's love in a way no one could imagine.

God kept his promise by sending Jesus to redeem us. The New Testament contains four books that tell us about Jesus' life and mission. They are the Gospels of Matthew, Mark, Luke, and John. The word *gospel* means "good news." The Gospels tell us the Good News that through Jesus' life, Death, and Resurrection, we can share in God's life of love forever.

Everything Jesus said and did leads us to God. Jesus explained: "I am the way and the truth and the life. No one comes to the Father except through me" (John 14:6).

---

# Activity

Jesus said he was the way, the truth, and the life. Write a synonym, or a word that means the same thing as another word, for each word Jesus used to describe himself.

Way _____

Truth _____

Life _____

How do the synonyms help you understand Jesus' words? Share your insight with a friend.

**The Church teaches and guides us.**

Through his life, Death, and Resurrection, Jesus made it possible for us to share in God's life of unending love and goodness. Jesus wants all of us to know this. Before he returned to his Father in heaven, Jesus gave his disciples a mission to share this Good News. He knew they would need strength and courage for this mission. He promised to send the Holy Spirit to help them. The Holy Spirit would be an advocate, or someone who speaks for someone else.

 *"The Advocate, the holy Spirit that the Father will send in my name—he will teach you everything and remind you of all that [I] told you. Peace I leave with you; my peace I give to you."*

*John 14:26–27*

## One Church, Many Cultures

The Church understands how important it is for people to read God's Word in a language they can understand. The Bible has been translated into more than six hundred languages, and it is one of the world's best-selling books! Bibles have been published in large print and in Braille as well. You can also find prayer cards that give prayers and Bible verses in English on one side and that give another language on the other side.

**Faith Word**

**Sacred Tradition** see p. 259

At Pentecost, the Holy Spirit came to the disciples, just as Jesus had promised. Peter and the other Apostles baptized about three thousand people on that day. The Church, first begun by Jesus, was sent on her mission on that day. The Apostles were strengthened by the Holy Spirit. The Spirit helped them to speak to everyone in his or her own language so that each person could understand the Good News. This helps us know that Christ's message is meant to be shared with all people.

The inspired teachings and prayers of the disciples have been handed down through the Church, all the way to the present day. We call these the Church's **Sacred Tradition**.

Sacred Tradition is how God reveals the Good News of Jesus in the prayers and practices of the Church. Tradition is not the Bible itself, but like the Bible, it is inspired by the Holy Spirit. Tradition includes teachings and practices handed down by Jesus and the Apostles. It includes creeds, or statements of our Christian beliefs. We pray the Nicene or Apostles' Creed at Mass. Tradition also includes Church teachings about how we worship God and share his love with others.

## Partners in Faith
### Saint Teresa of Ávila

Saint Teresa was a Spanish nun. She looked on God as a close friend. She said that we need to spend time with God to make our relationship grow, just as we have to spend time watering a garden to make it grow. Teresa was holy, intelligent, and lively; she loved music, dance, good conversation, and good books.

 **Learn more about the life of Saint Teresa of Ávila.**

## Faith Words

**Divine Revelation**

**Sacred Scripture**          **Sacred Tradition**

 **Show What You Know**

In your own words, give a short definition of each term.

**1. Divine Revelation**

_____

_____

_____

**2. Sacred Scripture**

_____

_____

_____

**3. Sacred Tradition**

_____

_____

_____

**4.** What is the difference between the Old and New Testaments
of the Bible?

_____

_____

_____

## Live Your Faith

• What parts of the Church's Sacred Tradition help you understand your faith?

_____

_____

• Describe ways to share the Good News of Jesus' life and work with others.

_____

_____

## Mini-Task

Extending an invitation is a way of letting someone know he or she is important to you. We send invitations for birthday parties as well as for parish celebrations such as Baptisms and weddings.

Inviting people to share our faith is an important part of being a disciple.

In the space below, design an invitation to Mass at your parish. Include key details such as the time and date of Mass and the important parts of the celebration. Share ways that the Mass helps us show God's love, such as praying and singing together.

_____

_____

_____

_____

 **Want to do more? Go to your Portfolio to continue this activity.**

## At Home

Discuss with your family members ways that the Good News has been passed on in your family.

# Who is God?

God is the Father, Son, and Holy Spirit. He is the one, true, and eternal God. God has created everything in the universe from nothing, and he keeps everything in existence. God is all-powerful and all-knowing. He is present in all times and places. Yet God is also our loving Father who has created us. God loves each one of us as his own children.

**Go to the digital portal for a prayer of adoration.**

*"Know, then, that the LORD, your God, is God: the faithful God who keeps covenant mercy to the thousandth generation toward those who love him and keep his commandments."*

*Deuteronomy 7:9*

## God has a loving plan for us.

We all make plans. We might plan what what we'll do tomorrow or where we'll play later today.

God is infinitely wise and infinitely good. He has a divine plan for all of creation. When you see leaves on trees changing from green to golden and hear them crunch under your feet, you can observe that the seasons have changed. You are using the gifts God gave you—your mind and senses—to help you understand something about God's loving plan for his creation.

You are an important part of God's plan. You are beautifully and wonderfully made. God has given you a body and a mind so you can understand and live in this world. God has also given you soul, an inner life that does not die. Your body, mind, and soul help you come to know God so that you can cooperate in his plan. God's plan is for all of us to live in communion with him forever.

**How do I know God?**

## Did You Know?

**There are different kinds of crosses.**

## Activity

God has a loving plan for creation. He calls us to help take care of his creation. Identify one general way you can do this. Fill out the chart showing steps you can take each day.

**I care for God's creation by:**

Day 1: _____.

Day 2: _____.

Day 3: _____.

Day 4: _____.

Day 5: _____.

## God reveals himself as Father, Son, and Holy Spirit.

God's love, power, goodness, and wisdom are a rich mystery, beyond the limits of our reason. But through faith we know that God is a Trinity: Three Persons in One God. There is God the Father, God the Son, and God the Holy Spirit. God has revealed himself in the Bible and in his creation.

Each Person of the Blessed Trinity is God. Each Person of the Trinity is unique. When we gather at Mass and profess our faith in God, we speak of our belief in God the Father almighty. This means that God has the power to do everything and anything. Nothing is more powerful than God.

We also say that God is the Creator of all things, both visible and invisible. This means that God has created both everything that we can see and everything that we cannot see, or even imagine. Nothing existed before God created everything. God alone has created everything out of love.

God has created us to share in the life of the Blessed Trinity. We live according to God's plan when we live in the love of the Father, the Son, and the Holy Spirit.

The Blessed Trinity is one God in three distinct Persons: Father, Son, and Holy Spirit. This is the central mystery of our faith and our life as Christians. When we say that God is eternal—has always existed and always will exist—we are speaking of all Three Persons of the Blessed Trinity.

When we say that God alone created everything out of love, we are speaking of the Blessed Trinity. When we say that God is always at work in his creation, we are speaking of the Blessed Trinity: the Father, the Son, and the Holy Spirit.

Humans cannot fully understand the Blessed Trinity, because God's mysterious, loving, and all-powerful nature is larger than our minds. One thing that we can know is that God loves us, because God is love. The Father, the Son, and the Holy Spirit share completely in an inner life of love and gift. We can see this love at work in God's plan for his creation and for all of us: God wants us to grow in love so that we can live in unity with him. When we imitate God's love, we grow closer to the Trinity.

We grow in God's eternal life and love.

## Jesus Christ is the Son of God, our Lord and Savior.

**Faith Word**

**Messiah** see p. 258

From the beginning, God has had a plan for us to live in his friendship. However, humans have often turned away from God by sinning. This did not divert or end God's plan. Instead, God promised to send a person who would save all people from sin so that everyone could live in God's friendship forever. Restoring our friendship with God is called *salvation*.

We read in the Bible that God promised to send a savior, or **messiah**. The word *messiah* means "anointed one." A person who is anointed has a special mission. The messiah sent by God had a mission to save God's people.

For many hundreds of years, God's people waited and prayed for the messiah to come. The prophet Isaiah gave people hope by telling them about the coming messiah. He described the messiah as the "Prince of Peace."

We know this messiah is our Savior and Lord, Jesus Christ. The name *Jesus* means "God saves." Jesus is God the Son, the Second Person of the Trinity. Jesus was born into the world and was like us in every way, except that he did not sin. When Jesus grew up, he revealed his mission at the synagogue one day.

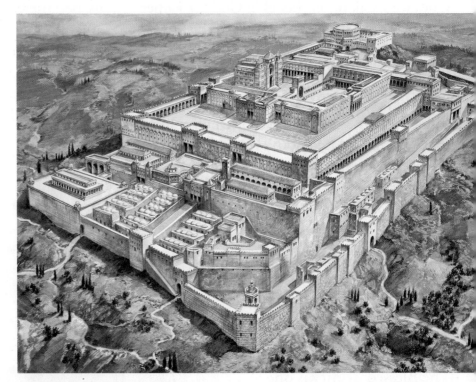

**The Temple in Jerusalem**

## What Makes Us Catholic?

Anointing with oil is a special sign in the Catholic Church. Chrism, or holy oil, is used in several sacraments. It is used in Baptism along with the Oil of Catechumens, as well as in Confirmation and Holy Orders. Chrism is made from olive oil and a sweet fragrance, often balsam. The Oil of the Sick is used to anoint the sick. Usually the oil for a diocese is blessed by the bishop at a special Mass in Holy Week. It is then given to parishes. Look for its use in sacraments at your church.

"He stood up to read and was handed a scroll of the prophet Isaiah. He unrolled the scroll and found the passage where it was written:

'The Spirit of the Lord is upon me,
    because he has anointed me
        to bring glad tidings to the poor.
He has sent me to proclaim liberty to captives
    and recovery of sight to the blind,
        to let the oppressed go free,
and to proclaim a year acceptable to the Lord.'

Rolling up the scroll, he handed it back to the attendant and sat down, and the eyes of all in the synagogue looked intently at him. He said to them, 'Today this scripture passage is fulfilled in your hearing'" (Luke 4:16–21).

Jesus showed everyone that he was sent by God the Father to fulfill his promises.

Through Jesus' life and teaching, we learn how to live in God's friendship. Jesus' Death and Resurrection has saved us from our sin. Jesus brings saving grace to all people so that we can live in the Trinity's love forever.

## One Church, Many Cultures

Catholic explorers and missionaries named countries, cities, and even mountains after Jesus. They did this to honor and thank God as they built communities for Christ in new lands. Some places named after Jesus are the Sangre de Cristo (Blood of Christ) mountains; Corpus Christi (Body of Christ), Texas; and El Salvador (the Savior), a country in Central America. These names all remind us of the power of Christ and the work of those explorers and missionaries, who wanted to share Christ's name and love with all people.

## Activity

The words and phrases below describe Jesus. Choose one and write a prayer using that word or phrase.

**Savior**          **Son of God**          **Lord**

**Christ**          **Good Shepherd**

Teach your prayer to a partner.

## The Holy Spirit guides and makes holy the Church.

After his Resurrection, Jesus appeared to his disciples many times over forty days, teaching them about God's Kingdom. Just before Jesus returned to his Father in heaven, he told the Apostles not to leave Jerusalem. He told them to "wait for 'the promise of the Father about which you have heard me speak; for John baptized with water, but in a few days you will be baptized with the holy Spirit'" (Acts of the Apostles 1:4–5).

The disciples did not completely understand what Jesus meant. They may have wondered: what was the "promise of the Father"? What did it mean to be baptized with the Holy Spirit?

Then, after Jesus ascended into heaven, his words were fulfilled. On the Jewish feast of Pentecost, the Apostles, with Mary and other disciples, had gathered to pray.

"And suddenly there came from the sky a noise like a strong driving wind, and it filled the entire house in which they were. Then there appeared to them tongues as of fire, which parted and came to rest on each one of them. And they were all filled with the holy Spirit" (Acts of the Apostles 2:2–4).

With the gifts of the Holy Spirit, the Apostles were able to go out and spread the Good News throughout the world. The Holy Spirit empowered them to go out and tell of Jesus' life, Death, and Resurrection. They preached and healed in Jesus' name. Through the centuries, the Holy Spirit has continued to guide and strengthen the Church. The Holy Spirit will guide the Church until the end of time. This is possible because our God is a living God who brings life and holiness to the Church through the Holy Spirit.

As members of the Church, we know that the Holy Spirit also guides each of us by helping us follow Jesus.

## Partners in Faith

### Saint Elizabeth of the Trinity

Elizabeth Catez was a French woman who loved the Trinity very much. She took the name of the Trinity when she became a nun. She said we can find God everywhere. She said she found God while praying, but also while cleaning up. Even when Elizabeth was sad, she praised God.

 **Learn more about the life of Saint Elizabeth of the Trinity.**

## Faith Word

**Messiah**

## ☑ Show What You Know

**In your own words, explain who the Blessed Trinity is.**

_____

_____

_____

**Why do we call Jesus the Messiah?**

_____

_____

_____

**What does it mean to be anointed?**

_____

_____

_____

## Live Your Faith

• The Holy Spirit guides the Church. What is the Holy Spirit guiding you to do?

_____

_____

_____

• What is something you can do this week to find out more about God's plan for your life?

_____

_____

_____

# Mini-Task

God created you for a purpose! Think about what makes you unique. What are your interests and gifts? In the God's Plan notebook below, describe three unique abilities that God has given to you. Then, at the bottom, write one way you use one or more of these gifts to share God's love with others.

**God's Plan**

_____

_____

_____

_____

_____

_____

_____

 **Want to do more? Go to your Portfolio to continue this activity.**

 **At Home**

Discuss with your family members ways that each of you has experienced the help and guidance of the Holy Spirit in your life.

# Why did God make us?

God made us to know, love, and serve him in this life and to be happy with him in the next life. He also made us to love one another. To help us, God has given us the gift of faith so that we can live in his love forever.

 **Go to the digital portal for a prayer of thanksgiving.**

*"For we walk by faith, not by sight."*
2 Corinthians 5:7

## God created us in his image and likeness.

People share many traits in common. Some are tall, some short, with curly or straight hair, different eye and skin colors, different heights. We may be girls or boys, athletes or artists. But we all share the same origin. Every human being is made in the image and likeness of God. In the Book of Genesis we read:

"God created mankind in his image; in the image of God he created them; male and female he created them" (Genesis 1:27).

Everything God created is good. Our goodness comes from God. This goodness gives each human person dignity—a special worth or honor. It is rooted in the reality that we are made in God's own image and likeness. The fact that God created us to love and serve him shows us how special we are to him. One way we can love God is by loving others.

> **What are some things I can see that I have in common with other people?**

## Did You Know?

 **We continue God's work by being stewards of creation.**

**Faith helps us respond to God's love.**

We are created by God, so we naturally seek him. This is the right thing to do, because we are meant to live in harmony and communion with God. This is what makes us happy, deep in our hearts. This is called faith.

God has given us the gift of faith to help us seek and believe in him. Faith means that we believe in God's goodness and love. Faith gives us trust that what God wants for us is good for us. Faith says "yes" to God when he asks us to make choices.

## Activity

Faith in God is a gift. We cannot earn it, but we can ask for it. What would you say to someone who doesn't have the gift of faith? Role-play this talk with a friend.

## One Church, Many Cultures

**K**nowing different languages helps us listen to, care for, and pray with others who may not speak our own language, both at Church and in our communities. Ask friends or classmates who speak more than one language to tell you how to say "yes" in a different language. Or, choose one of the ways to say "yes" below.

- **In Spanish: sí**
- **In French: oui**
- **In Tagalog: oo**
- **In Japanese: hai**
- **In Polish: tak**
- **In Hawaiian: 'ae**

## Grace helps us live in friendship with the Blessed Trinity.

God has created us in his own image. In this sense, each of us is created to be good. However, because of Original Sin, humans suffer many ill effects. One effect could be a distorted fear of God, which leads to distrust of him. Another may be that, instead of happily making decisions based on reason and conscience, we tend to want what feels easiest or most pleasant. Another could be that we tend to see our neighbor more as a threat than as someone to love.

In the Old Testament book of Genesis, we read about God's love for two people we know as Adam and Eve. They were happy and had everything they needed, because they lived in God's friendship and in a state of original holiness. One day they faced a choice. They could follow or disobey God's command not to eat from the Tree of Knowledge of Good and Evil. Adam and Eve chose to disobey. They

**Faith Word**

**grace** see p. 257

said "no" to God. When they made this choice, they turned away from God's friendship and lost the holy and happy life they had with him.

We call this first sin Original Sin. It is not something that we have done, but it is passed down to all human beings. Original Sin inclines us to commit personal sins. A sin is a choice to go against God's will. Sin hurts our friendship with God. Sin keeps us from living the holy and happy life God has planned for us.

Despite our sin, God never stops loving us and never gives up on us. In the account of Adam and Eve, we learn that even though they turned away from God, God did not turn away from them. Instead, God showed them mercy. God always gives us the **grace** to live in his friendship. Grace is our share in God's life and love.

## What Makes Us Catholic?

Our Church understands that we receive different kinds of grace from God. *Sanctifying grace* is a permanent gift we receive to help us be holy and share in God's life. *Actual grace* is a temporary gift that helps us understand what to do in situations as they are happening. It tells us how to act as God wants and make the right decisions according to his will for us. Actual grace gives us the strength to turn away from sin. *Sacramental grace* is the grace we receive in the sacraments. Each sacrament gives us its own particular grace.

## We are called to live as Jesus' faithful disciples.

God invites us to live in friendship with him now and forever, even after our earthly lives are over. Jesus once told a parable to help us understand this.

"A man gave a great dinner to which he invited many. When the time for the dinner came, he dispatched his servant to say to those invited, 'Come, everything is now ready.' But one by one, they all began to excuse themselves'" (Luke 14:16–18).

Sadly, some people do not accept the invitation to live in God's love. They freely choose to separate themselves from God's love by committing serious sin. The state of living apart from God forever is called hell.

But when we accept God's love, God does everything possible to lead us toward eternal life with him. He has given us the gift of faith. He strengthens us with his grace in the sacraments. He leads us toward eternal life with him. Even after we die, God shows his love and mercy to us.

Sometimes, people are not fully ready to enter God's Kingdom. Their sins prevent them from fully participating in God's love. Those sins need to be purged. This is a state of being we call Purgatory. God does all of this because he loves us so much.

We can act on God's gifts every day, by living faithful lives as Christ's followers. This is how we accept God's invitation to the eternal life of peace, joy, and friendship.

## Activity

A sin is a choice not to trust God. Consider the following sins. Write ways they go against trust in God.

Disobey parents

Tell a lie

Steal

Cheat on a test

Now write a way that you can show trust in God instead of sinning.

_____

_____

_____

_____

_____

_____

_____

_____

"'Come, you who are blessed by my Father. Inherit the kingdom prepared for you from the foundation of the world. For I was hungry and you gave me food, I was thirsty and you gave me drink, a stranger and you welcomed me, naked and you clothed me, ill and you cared for me, in prison and you visited me.' Then the righteous will answer him and say, 'Lord, when did we see you hungry and feed you, or thirsty and give you drink? When did we see you a stranger and welcome you, or naked and clothe you? When did we see you ill or in prison, and visit you?' And the king will say to them in reply, 'Amen, I say to you, whatever you did for one of these least brothers of mine, you did for me'" (Matthew 25:34–40).

Jesus gives us the Holy Spirit to strengthen us to do this work. With God's help, we are able to live the way Jesus wants us to live.

During his life, Jesus taught us how to respond to God's invitation to trust and love him. He explained that everything we do for others, we do for God. He explained that this was part of God's plan from the beginning of the world. He said that when he comes again in glory, he will say:

## Partners in Faith
### Saints Louis and Zélie Martin

Louis and Zélie Martin lived in France. They understood that God was calling them to become holy by loving each other. They both worked hard to support their family: Louis made watches, and Zélie made lace. Their family prayed together daily, celebrated their joys, and supported one another. Louis was heartbroken when Zélie died. Five of their daughters became nuns, including their youngest, Saint Thérèse of Lisieux. Louis and Zélie are the first married couple to be canonized at the same time.

 **Learn more about the lives of Saints Louis and Zélie Martin.**

## Faith Word

**grace**

 **Show What You Know**

Use the Word Bank to complete the sentences.

**creation     grace     communion     faith**

1. We live in _____ with God when we respect his _____ and the special dignity of all human beings.

2. _____ helps us trust that what God wants for us is good for us.

3. _____ is the gift of God's life in us that helps us live in God's goodness and holiness.

## Live Your Faith

- What is God's special mission for humans? What steps are you taking on your mission from God?

_____

_____

_____

_____

_____

_____

_____

- In what ways can you prepare for eternal life with God now?

_____

_____

_____

_____

_____

_____

_____

_____

## Mini-Task

There is a lot of noise in our busy world. It is easy to forget that an important part of friendship is listening. Prayer includes both talking and listening to God.

Interview a friend to find out his or her answers to the following questions. Add your own question to the list.

Listen carefully to your friend's responses. Record your friend's answers on the lines below.

1. What do you like to do for fun?

   _____

   _____

2. Who has shown you how to be a good friend?

   _____

   _____

3. Who has taught you about Jesus?

   _____

   _____

4. 

   _____

   _____

 **Want to do more? Go to your Portfolio to continue this activity.**

Families help one another choose to love and do good. What is one thing you can do as a family this week to live God's mission?

# Who is Jesus Christ?

Jesus is the only begotten Son of God. He is also the son of Mary. He is both true God and true man. How can this be possible? We know that with God, all things are possible. With Jesus, we can live the life God wants for us.

**Go to the digital portal for a *Lectio* and *Visio Divina* prayer.**

*"It is truly right . . . to give you thanks,*
*Father most holy,*
*through your beloved Son  Jesus Christ,*
*your Word through whom you made all things,*
*whom you sent as our Savior and Redeemer,*
*incarnate by the Holy Spirit and born of the Virgin."*

*Eucharistic Prayer 2, Roman Missal*

**Mary was conceived without Original Sin.**

God's plan is for all people to live in communion with him forever. Mary was part of God's plan. God chose Mary to be the mother of his Son. God prepared Mary in a special way. She was "full of grace," which means the moment of her conception in her mother's womb, Mary was free from Original Sin and its effects. We call this truth the **Immaculate Conception.** Mary was not weakened by sin and chose not to commit sin all through her life.

Although Mary did not sin, she faced suffering and sadness in her life. Still, her faith in God remained strong. When she was asked by God to be the mother of his Son, Mary responded by saying "yes" to God.

**Faith Word**

**Immaculate Conception**
see p. 258

 **Hail Mary**

**What Makes Us Catholic?**

Catholics attend Mass on Sundays. We also go to Mass on certain feast days called Holy Days of Obligation. On Holy Days of Obligation, we join others in our Church to celebrate and honor Jesus, Mary, and the saints.

**What does God ask of me?**

# Did You Know?

 **We celebrate Mary throughout the year.**

## Activity

Look up the feast day of the Immaculate Conception on your church calendar. We say that Mary is the Immaculate Conception because she was free from Original Sin. Explain to a friend what that means.

## Jesus teaches us how to live.

God sent his only Son, Jesus, into the world to live among us. The Incarnation is the truth that the Son of God became man. Jesus is both human and divine. He is the Son of God and the son of Mary. In the Gospels, we read that Jesus grew up in Nazareth with his mother, Mary, and with his foster father, Joseph. Jesus loved and respected his human family. Mary and Joseph shared their Jewish faith with Jesus, and they taught him to pray according to their custom.

When Jesus was about 30 years old, he began his public ministry in towns near where he lived. He taught people about God in a way that no one had before. Jesus called God "Abba." The word *abba* is a loving way of saying "Father."

All through his life and in his teaching, Jesus showed us how to live in God's holiness and happiness. He did this through his words and actions. He helped those who were poor or sick. He cared for the lonely. He treated everyone with fairness and respect.

When people heard Jesus' teachings, many were interested in what he had to say. Jesus invited them to learn more by following him. Many said "yes" to this invitation. We know them as Jesus' disciples.

Jesus spent about three years with his disciples teaching, healing, and helping others. Jesus asked them to live as *he* did, spreading God the Father's message of love.

**Because of Jesus' Death and Resurrection, we can have eternal life.**

**Faith Word**

**Resurrection** see p. 259

Jesus' suffering and Death is the greatest sacrifice anyone has ever made. Jesus died for our sins. His Death and **Resurrection** are the most effective signs of God's love for us. When we understand that Jesus is both human and divine, we know that his suffering was real. This truth highlights how deeply God loves us: he chose to sacrifice himself to open the gates of heaven for us. This truth highlights how deeply God loves us: he chose to sacrifice himself to open the gates of heaven for us.

| Jesus chooses love. | At his Last Supper, Jesus gave his Apostles his Body and Blood under the appearance of bread and wine. Jesus explained to the disciples: "No one has greater love than this, to lay down one's life for one's friends" (John 15:13). |
|---|---|
| Jesus prays. | After Jesus shared this last meal with his Apostles, he went to the garden to pray to his Father. He said: "Father, if you are willing, take this cup away from me; still, not my will but yours be done" (Luke 22:42). Jesus knew what was going to happen to him, yet he accepted his Father's will. |
| Jesus forgives. | As Jesus was on the Cross, he showed us how to forgive others. Even though he was in terrible pain and suffering, Jesus forgave the people who mocked him and hurt him. He said: "Father, forgive them, they know not what they do" (Luke 23:34). |

After Jesus died on the Cross, his disciples placed his body in a tomb. A heavy stone was rolled across the entrance of the tomb.

On the morning of the third day after Jesus' Death, some of his disciples went to the tomb. They saw that the stone had been rolled away. Jesus' body was gone. Two angels told them that Jesus had been raised from the dead.

The mystery of Jesus being raised from the dead is called the Resurrection. By his Death and Resurrection, Jesus gained our salvation and brought us the hope of eternal life in heaven.

## One Church, Many Cultures

**T**he Church's Holy Week celebrates and remembers the events that happened during Jesus' final days before his Death, including his Resurrection. In some countries, the week includes processions on Palm Sunday and Good Friday. Latin American Catholics sometimes spread colorful carpets called *alfombras* on the ground for these processions. These carpets show religious images beside native designs of flowers or animals. In many countries, Catholics participate in the Way of the Cross, a procession similar to the Stations of the Cross, or they participate in short pilgrimages to holy sites. Italian Catholics walk to the Colosseum in Rome on Good Friday to remember the early Christians who were martyred there.

## Activity

Look at the picture of the women visiting the empty tomb. Imagine that you were there. What are you thinking? How do you feel? Write down your thoughts.

_____

_____

_____

_____

_____

_____

_____

_____

_____

_____

## Jesus will come again at the end of time.

After his Resurrection, Jesus appeared to his disciples several times over forty days. He wanted his disciples to believe all that he had said and done. His Resurrection was proof that he was the Messiah, the Son of God. Seeing Jesus raised from the dead encouraged the disciples to continue his mission. Finally, the Risen Christ took his disciples to a mountain. Jesus blessed his disciples and then ascended to his Father in heaven.

Jesus will come again in glory at the end of time. He will judge all people. This is called the **Last Judgment** (see Matthew 25:31–46). We will be judged by our works and by the choices we have made with the gift of faith God has given us. We hope for Christ's coming in the future, and we prepare by being faithful to him and living in friendship and peace every day of our lives.

**Faith Word**

**Last Judgment** see p. 258

## Partners in Faith
### Saint Timothy

Saint Timothy's mother and grandmother taught him about Jesus. Timothy met Saint Paul and became his close friend. He traveled with Paul even though he was never very healthy. Timothy helped Paul write his epistles. When Timothy was the bishop of Ephesus, his faith gave him the courage to die for Jesus.

 **Learn more about the life of Saint Timothy.**

**Faith Words**

Immaculate Conception    Resurrection

Last Judgment

## ☑ Show What You Know

Circle the correct answer for each sentence.

1. The teaching that Mary was free from Original Sin from the very first moment of her life is called the _____.

   a. Annunciation

   b. Immaculate Conception

   c. Assumption

2. The _____ is the mystery of Jesus being raised from the dead and to new life.

   a. Resurrection

   b. Judgment

   c. Rising

3. At the _____, Jesus will come in great glory to judge all people by their works and the choices they made.

   a. Last Supper

   b. Last Eucharist

   c. Last Judgment

## Live Your Faith

• Mary said "yes" to God. In what ways are you doing what God asks?

_____

_____

• Jesus showed us how to live in the way he prayed, forgave people, and chose love. Which of these things is hardest to do? In what ways do *you* do it?

_____

_____

_____

## How does Jesus Christ show me how to live?

# Mini-Task

The Gospels are filled with Jesus' teachings and actions. In some ways, they are like an instruction manual for life. Instruction manuals often include text, pictures, and/or diagrams to help us along the way.

Compose a text message that would help someone know how to follow Jesus. Use text or images (such as emojis) in your text message.

 **Want to do more? Go to your Portfolio to continue this activity.**

Mary, the mother of Jesus, faced sadness in her life. In what ways does your family help you when you are feeling sad or alone?

# What is the Church?

The Church is the Body of Christ, and we are her members. We are joined to Christ and to one another by our Baptism. As members of the Church, we bring the light of Christ to the world by our faithful, loving actions.

 **Go to the digital portal for a prayer of blessing.**

*"Just so, your light must shine before others, that they may see your good deeds and glorify your heavenly Father."*

*Matthew 5:16*

## The Church is the Body of Christ.

To understand the Church, it is helpful to think about the Mass. When we go to Mass, we see many different people. We see the priest, deacons, extraordinary ministers of Holy Communion, lectors, servers, ushers, and the assembly, or faithful people. At Mass, God's people gather in the name of the Father, the Son, and the Holy Spirit. Each person takes an active part in the Church's mission to bring Christ to the world.

Lectors bring Christ to us by proclaiming God's Word in Sacred Scripture. The priest consecrates the bread and wine so that, through the Holy Spirit, they become Christ's Body and Blood. Priests, deacons, and extraordinary ministers of Holy Communion bring the Body and Blood of Jesus Christ in the Sacrament of the Eucharist to the people. Strengthened by Christ's Body and Blood, all of God's people are called to go out and bring Christ to the whole world.

The Mass is celebrated all over the world. It is celebrated in big churches called cathedrals, where thousands of people might gather. It is celebrated in small chapels, with just a few people. When we see God's people all around us at Mass, we can know that there are millions more celebrating the same mystery with us. Although we are many, we are one Body in Christ.

How will I bring Christ to the world today?

## Did You Know?

 **Church buildings reflect who we are.**

## We are called to share the Good News of Jesus.

Our Baptism makes us members of the Church. Because the Church is the Body of Christ on earth, her membership is unlike anything else. We are joined to Christ and to one another in a holy and powerful way. This is the Gift of the Holy Spirit we receive at our Baptism, and it is how we share in God's life and holiness.

The work of the Church is supported by all of the baptized people working in communion with one another in a mystical way. Saint Paul explained that just as a body has many different parts, the Church does, too. Each of us has something to do in the Church.

For example, some men and women enter **religious life** by becoming religious sisters, brothers, or priests. As members of religious communities, they make vows, or promises, to God. These vows are chastity, poverty, and obedience. In their communities, these men and women share their goods, their time, their prayer, and their lives. They are free to serve God and their neighbors. They are not distracted by any need for material things, power, or fame.

The **laity** are baptized members of the Church who share in the Church's mission to bring the Good News to the world. They are also known as laypeople or the Christian faithful. You do not have to wait to be an adult to be an active member of the Church. You can find ways to share the Good News at home among your family. You can take part in parish celebrations and the sacraments. At school, whenever you play fair, tell the truth, or act with kindness toward others, you are shining Christ's light for all.

## Faith Words

**religious life** see p. 258

**laity** see p. 258

## Activity

Each of us has something to do in the Church. Name a way each of the following people serves the Church.

lector _____

bishop _____

religious _____

pope _____

priest _____

catechist _____

Write two ways you can serve the Church.

_____

_____

_____

_____

## The Holy Spirit helps us carry on the mission of the Church.

Jesus spread the message of God's love everywhere he went. This was Jesus' work, or mission. He asked his disciples to do the same. After Jesus' Ascension, when he returned to his Father in heaven, the disciples continued Jesus' work. Their mission was to share the Good News of Jesus Christ. This is how they carried out their mission:

• They told others the Good News that Jesus is the Son of God, who died and rose to save us from sin.

• They baptized those who heard and believed the Good News.

• They gathered together to praise God and to celebrate the Eucharist.

• They showed by their words and actions that God's love was active in their lives and in the world.

• They reached out to the poor and healed the sick and suffering.

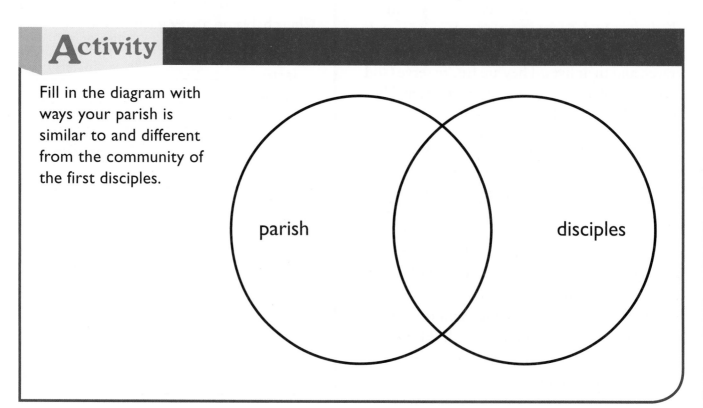

## Activity

Fill in the diagram with ways your parish is similar to and different from the community of the first disciples.

parish          disciples

The mission of the disciples is the mission of the Church today. We are called to continue this work.

The Catholic Church includes many people in many countries around the world. We are all ages, personalities, nationalities, and races. We have different backgrounds, cultures, and languages. But all Catholics around the world share the same beliefs in Jesus and the Church.

We celebrate the same sacraments and follow the Ten Commandments. We are united by our Baptism, which joins us to Christ and all members of the Church. We receive Christ's Body and Blood in the Eucharist. We are strengthened and led by the Holy Spirit to carry out Christ's mission. This is the fullness of the Catholic faith. The word *catholic* means "universal." The Catholic Church is universal and open to all people.

The Catholic Church recognizes and respects all religions. We work together with other Christians to witness or declare the message of Jesus to the world. We respect people of other faiths. We respect their freedom as we share our beliefs and do our best to understand theirs. We are friends with people of all faiths as we try to make the world a better place for everyone.

## One Church, Many Cultures

**N**o matter where we are in the world, the Catholic Church celebrates the same Mass. There may be different music or other expressions of our faith, but that faith remains the same. Chinese Catholics may include elements of Tibetan chants in the liturgy, while Danish Catholics celebrate a quiet, calm service that connects to the popular Danish customs of *hygge*, or comfort. Guitar music is important in the Latin American Church, and Catholics in Israel are able to celebrate the Mass in Hebrew, deepening the Church's connection to the Jewish faith of the Old Testament. The worldwide Church always worships together, even when we do so differently.

## The pope and bishops serve the Church.

Jesus sent out his Apostles to share the Good News and make disciples of all nations. That is why we say the Church is apostolic.

The direct successors of the Apostles are bishops. They lead local communities of the Church called dioceses. The direct authority of the Apostles has been handed down to the bishops through each generation. Bishops continue the work Jesus gave to the Apostles. They act in Jesus' name. They govern, or lead, the faithful. They sanctify us by celebrating the sacraments, praying, and preaching. *To sanctify* means "to make holy."

The pope is the Bishop of Rome, in Italy. He continues the leadership of the Apostle Peter and works with the bishops as their leader. Together with the bishops, he leads and guides the whole Church. Their leadership helps the Church continue her mission.

### What Makes Us Catholic?

When Jesus said to Saint Peter "Upon this rock, I will build my church" (Matthew 16:18), Peter became the first pope. Since then, there has been an unbroken line of popes. Many popes have shared the Catholic faith in new and exciting ways through travel and new forms of communication. The popes reflect the time in which they work, but they all have one goal in common: to proclaim the Good News of Jesus Christ.

### Partners in Faith
#### Saint Kateri Tekakwitha

Kateri was an Algonquin-Mohawk woman. She caught smallpox when she was a child. The disease left her with scars and weak eyesight. But she could still see the important things. When Kateri was baptized at age 19, she decided she wanted to live the rest of her life for Jesus. She is the first Native American to be named a saint.

 **Learn more about the life of Saint Kateri Tekakwitha.**

## Faith Words

**religious life      laity**

 ## Show What You Know

Read the statements. Circle whether the statement is True or False.
Correct any false statements you find.

**1.** The Church's mission is to bring Christ to the world. True / False _____

_____

_____

**2.** The pope and bishops lead and serve the Church. True / False _____

_____

_____

**3.** Men and women who make vows to God and share everything for the
common good are called part of the laity. True / False _____

_____

_____

## Live Your Faith

• What work can you do as part of the laity?

_____

_____

_____

_____

_____

• The Church works together with other Christians to witness the message
of Jesus to the world. In what ways can you be friends with people of all faiths?

_____

_____

_____

_____

_____

## Mini-Task

"We can do small things with great love."

This famous phrase is attributed to Saint Teresa of Calcutta.

In what ways can this quote remind us of what it means to be a member of a team or community? Turn to and talk with a partner.

What is a need that you see in your family, classroom, or parish?

What are some small things that could be done to help meet the need you identified?

Prioritize your list of "small things" by highlighting what should be done first.

Then answer the following questions.

| need |
| --- |
| |

| small things |
| --- |
| |

What people are needed for this "small thing"? _____

What research must be done? _____

What materials are needed? _____

Other considerations: _____

 **Want to do more? Go to your Portfolio to continue this activity.**

# At Home

Renewing baptismal promises is a good way to renew faith.
Light a candle and renew your promises as a family.

How do we celebrate what we believe?

# Unit 2
## The Faith Celebrated

Community of Believers

# Unit Prayer

**Leader:** Saint Teresa of Ávila knew how important it is for us to celebrate God's love. She prayed: "May you use those gifts you received and pass on the love that has been given to you." We must not hide God's love that fills our hearts, and we must use our gifts to let the world know of this love.

Let us listen to how missionary disciples among us celebrate the love of God.

**Leader:** Let us pray:

O God, help us to be open to your Holy Spirit, that we celebrate your love for us in all we do.

**Reader:** That we celebrate your love in our minds;

**All:** help us share your love with all.

**Reader:** That we celebrate your love in our hearts;

**All:** help us share your love with all.

**Reader:** That we celebrate your love in all we say and do;

**All:** help us share your love with all.

**Reader:** That we celebrate Jesus' gift of love at Mass;

**All:** help us share your love with all.

*End the Unit Prayer by singing the song for this unit.*

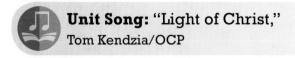

**Unit Song:** "Light of Christ," Tom Kendzia/OCP

## Missionary Discipleship

How have you celebrated God's love with your family and friends? Was there a part of Mass that helped you want to "sing, dance, and praise" God? Did you feel closer to God?

# How does God share his life with us?

We were created to share in God's own life. Jesus gave the Church seven sacred signs called sacraments to share God's life with us. In the sacraments, the Holy Spirit gives us grace to help us live as followers of Jesus.

**Go to the digital portal for a prayer of adoration.**

*"Jesus said to him, 'I am the way and the truth and the life. . . . If you know me, then you will also know my Father.'"*

*John 14:6–7*

## Jesus is the Head of the Church.

When you walk into church, what is the first thing you notice? For most Catholics, it is a crucifix, an image of Jesus on the Cross. Of course, this is only a symbol of Jesus. This symbol of Jesus reminds us that the Risen Christ leads his Church.

We may not be able to see Jesus the way we can see the priest, lector, servers, and other people who participate in the Mass. But in the liturgy, we gather with Jesus' whole Church. This includes all baptized people, on earth and in heaven. We are one in the Body of Christ.

After his Ascension, Jesus explained this to a man named Saul. Saul had been persecuting Jesus' followers, meaning he singled them out for mistreatment because of their faith. One day Saul was traveling.

"A light from the sky suddenly flashed around him. He fell to the ground and heard a voice saying to him, 'Saul, Saul, why are you persecuting me?' He said, 'Who are you, sir?' The reply came, 'I am Jesus, whom you are persecuting'" (Acts of the Apostles 9:3–5).

Jesus was telling Saul that by mistreating Jesus' followers, he also mistreated Jesus. Jesus loved his followers then, and Jesus loves us now. The next time you are at Mass, remember that you and everyone around you form the Body of Christ. We are one in Christ our Savior.

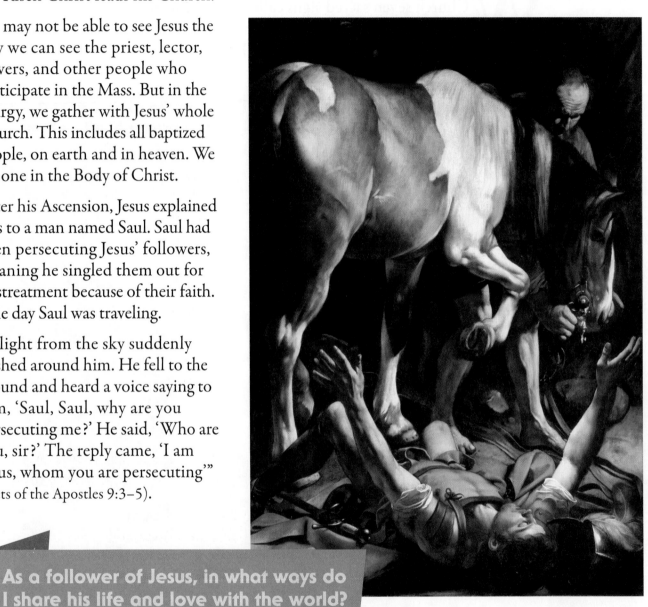

As a follower of Jesus, in what ways do I share his life and love with the world?

## Did You Know?

**In special circumstances, Mass may be celebrated outside of a church.**

## The Holy Spirit prepares us to celebrate the Church's liturgy.

How can it be possible for so many people to be the Body of Christ? The power of the Holy Spirit brings us together in this way. When we come together in Christ's name for the liturgy, the Holy Spirit is with us. We see this throughout the two main parts of the Mass, the Liturgy of the Word and the Liturgy of the Eucharist.

During the **Liturgy of the Word**, we listen to what God is saying to us in the Scripture readings. The Holy Spirit prepares our hearts to hear and understand how Christ lives and acts in us right now.

In the **Liturgy of the Eucharist**, we celebrate Jesus' saving actions in his suffering, Death, and Resurrection. We are united to Jesus. Through the power of the Holy Spirit and the action of the priest, our gifts of bread and wine become the Body and Blood of Christ during the eucharistic prayer called the Consecration. The Risen Jesus is fully present to us in the Eucharist. This is called the Real Presence.

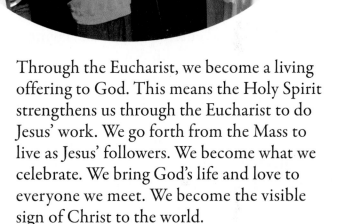

### Faith Words

**Liturgy of the Word** see p. 258

**Liturgy of the Eucharist** see p. 258

Through the Eucharist, we become a living offering to God. This means the Holy Spirit strengthens us through the Eucharist to do Jesus' work. We go forth from the Mass to live as Jesus' followers. We become what we celebrate. We bring God's life and love to everyone we meet. We become the visible sign of Christ to the world.

## Activity

The Mass has two main parts. Work in small groups to fill out the chart with all you know about each part. Discuss why both parts are important.

| Liturgy of the Word | Liturgy of the Eucharist |
| --- | --- |
|  |  |
|  |  |
|  |  |
|  |  |

## We receive God's grace through the sacraments.

In the Bible, we read about Saul, who was persecuting followers of Jesus. He was traveling to the city of Damascus when there was a great flash in the sky. Saul fell to the ground. Jesus had something to say to Saul. He wanted to show Saul how much he loved him. But Jesus' love was so great, Saul wasn't able to see it. Still, the Lord had plans for Saul. He sent a man named Ananias to him. Saul's account continues:

"Saul got up from the ground, but when he opened his eyes he could see nothing; so they led him by the hand and brought him to Damascus. For three days he was unable to see, and he neither ate nor drank. . . . So Ananias went and entered the house; laying his hands on him, he said, 'Saul, my brother, the Lord has sent me, Jesus who appeared to you on the way by which you came, that you may regain your sight and be filled with the holy Spirit.' Immediately things like scales fell from his eyes and he regained his sight. He got up and was baptized" (Acts of the Apostles 9:8–9, 17–18).

## What Makes Us Catholic?

The Holy Spirit prepares us to receive the grace of the sacraments. But we prepare ourselves to celebrate the sacraments themselves as well. If we have committed a serious sin, we must celebrate the Sacrament of Reconciliation before we celebrate the Eucharist. We do not eat or drink anything except water or medicine for one hour before we receive the Eucharist. Before we celebrate Confirmation, we choose a Confirmation name and a sponsor, celebrate the Sacrament of Reconciliation, and perform works of service. This preparation means our hearts and minds are clear, open, and ready to receive the grace of each sacrament.

Ananias laid his hands on Saul in Jesus' name. Jesus wants us to see, touch, hear, and even taste his great love for us. He has given us seven sacred signs of his grace and love, which we call sacraments. The sacraments give God's grace to Jesus' presence with us.

Through the Holy Spirit, we receive God's sanctifying grace in the sacraments. As God's life grows in us, we become more like Jesus. We are able to spread the message of God's love and live in his friendship.

| **Sacraments of Christian Initiation**<br><br>Baptism, Confirmation, Eucharist | These sacraments welcome us into the Church. They strengthen us to be followers of Jesus, and they nourish our faith. |
| --- | --- |
| **Sacraments of Healing**<br><br>Penance and Reconciliation, Anointing of the Sick | These sacraments offer us God's forgiveness, peace, and healing. They strengthen and encourage us. |
| **Sacraments at the Service of Communion**<br><br>Holy Orders, Matrimony | These sacraments celebrate particular ways of serving God and the Church. They strengthen those who receive them so they will be faithful. |

## Activity

Write one or two ways that you experience one of your senses in the sacraments or at Mass.

Five senses: hearing, sight, touch, smell, taste

_____

_____

_____

_____

**Sacramental signs and actions help us share in God's grace.**

Actions that can help us share in God's grace. These are called **sacramentals**.

The word *sacramental* sounds like *sacrament*, but the two words are different.

The sacraments give us God's grace. Sacramentals prepare us to receive God's grace. They are signs we can touch, see, and hear. Sacramentals help us live and act on the sacraments. For example, when most of us think of the Sacrament of Baptism, we think of water. In the Sacrament of Baptism, water clearly shows that Original Sin is being washed away as the words of the rite are spoken. The sacrament cleanses us of Original Sin and of any personal sin, moving us from death to new life in Christ. When we bless ourselves with holy water, we are reminded of our Baptism. Holy water used this way is a sacramental.

Sacramentals are sacred signs. They help prepare us to receive and act on sacramental grace.

**Faith Word**

sacramentals see p. 259

## One Church, Many Cultures

**M**any Latino Catholics pray and reflect on their faith using candles, especially candles placed inside glass containers that are painted with colorful images of the Blessed Virgin Mary, of Christ on the Cross, or of saints of the Church. These candles, called *veladoras*, can be used at home or in church. They are often found in front of statues of Mary and the saints. Some Catholics pray before these candles to ask a particular saint for his or her intercession, or to request help from God through prayer.

## Partners in Faith

### Saint John Paul II

Saint John Paul II was pope for twenty-five years. During that time, people were worried about many things. He said: "Be not afraid!" He told them that what really matters is that God loves us and that we love God. Saint John Paul II loved the Rosary and added the Luminous Mysteries to the prayer.

 **Learn more about the life of Saint John Paul II.**

## Faith Words

**Liturgy of the Word**

**Liturgy of the Eucharist**      **sacramentals**

 **Show What You Know**

In your own words, write definitions for the terms.

**Liturgy of the Word**

_____

_____

_____

_____

**Liturgy of the Eucharist**

_____

_____

_____

_____

**sacramentals**

_____

_____

_____

_____

## Live Your Faith

• After Mass, we are told to "go forth" and live as Jesus' followers.
  In what ways can you do this next Sunday?

_____

_____

• What do you need the strength of the sacraments to help you do now?

_____

_____

_____

How can I prepare my heart to celebrate God's love?

## Mini-Task

Part of being a responsible student is being prepared.

What are some ways you prepare for school? On the checklist marked School, write three or four things you do to get ready each day.

Think about ways the items in your checklist prepare you to learn. Share your ideas with a partner.

We prepare ourselves to celebrate the liturgy.

What are some ways you prepare for Mass? On the checklist marked Mass, write three or four things you do to get ready for Mass.

Share your checklist with a partner.

| School |
|--------|
| ☐ _____ |
| ☐ _____ |
| ☐ _____ |
| ☐ _____ |

| Mass |
|------|
| ☐ _____ |
| ☐ _____ |
| ☐ _____ |
| ☐ _____ |

 **Want to do more? Go to your Portfolio to continue this activity.**

 **At Home**

Pictures, rosaries, holy cards, and crosses are all sacramentals. They help prepare us to receive God's grace. What sacramentals do you have in your home or remember from church or school?

## How do we praise and thank God?

God has given us so much that we want to thank him all year long. The liturgical year helps us. It guides us through the seasons of our Church year. It helps us remember and celebrate our great feasts. Our liturgy gives us a glimpse of the joy and holiness of the eternal celebration we will share with Jesus and all the saints forever.

 **Go to the digital portal for a traditional prayer.**

*"Praise the LORD, my soul;*
*I will praise the LORD all my life,*
*sing praise to my God while I live."*

Psalm 146:2

## The Church's feasts and seasons celebrate Jesus' work of salvation.

Jesus wants us to celebrate together. In fact, Jesus' first miracle took place at a celebration.

"On the third day there was a wedding in Cana in Galilee, and the mother of Jesus was there. Jesus and his disciples were also invited to the wedding. When the wine ran short, the mother of Jesus said to him, 'They have no wine.' [And] Jesus said to her, 'Woman, how does your concern affect me? My hour has not yet come.' His mother said to the servers, 'Do whatever he tells you.' Now there were six stone water jars there. . . . Jesus told them, 'Fill the jars with water.' So they filled them to the brim. Then he told them, 'Draw some out now and take it to the headwaiter.' So they took it. And when the headwaiter tasted the water that had become wine, without knowing where it came from, . . . the headwaiter called the bridegroom and said to him, 'Everyone serves good wine first, and then when people have drunk freely, an inferior one; but you have kept the good wine until now.' Jesus did this as the beginning of his signs in Cana in Galilee and so revealed his glory, and his disciples began to believe in him" (John 2:1–11).

How do I feel when I am thankful?

## Did You Know?

**The Church celebrates feasts and holy days every year.**

With this miracle, Jesus shows us how important it is to celebrate together. As members of the Church, we celebrate God's love with great feasts. We gather together with our whole Church family. We do this in the liturgy. In the liturgy, the Church, through the Holy Spirit, participates in the prayer and saving work of Jesus. It includes the celebration of the Mass and the sacraments. It also includes the Liturgy of the Hours. This is a special prayer of the Church that is prayed several times during the day.

Our most important liturgical celebration is Sunday Mass. We call Sunday the Lord's Day. It is the day that Jesus Christ rose from the dead to save us. On Sundays, we gather with the Church for the celebration of the Mass. We adore and praise God, thanking him for his many gifts. We celebrate Jesus' life, Death, Resurrection, and Ascension. The Mass is also called the celebration of the Eucharist. *Eucharist* means "thanksgiving."

## Activity

Imagine you are a guest at the wedding feast at Cana. On the lines below, retell the account of Jesus changing water into wine. Be sure to include how the wedding guests reacted to Jesus' miracle.

_____

_____

_____

_____

_____

_____

**The liturgical year guides us as we worship God and honor Mary and the saints.**

Our celebrations of the liturgy are so important that we mark the Church year by them. We call this the **liturgical year**. Throughout the liturgical year, we remember and celebrate Jesus' birth, life, Death, Resurrection, and Ascension. We celebrate the different Church seasons with readings, songs, prayers, and even colors. The liturgical year begins in late November or early December, with the season of Advent. It ends with the Feast of Christ the King.

In every liturgical season, we honor Mary, the Mother of Jesus, with special feast days. The Church is devoted to Mary because she is the Mother of the Son of God. She is our Mother and the Mother of the Church, too. Mary is the best example of how to live as a disciple of Jesus. On her feast days, we remember the ways God blessed Mary. We recall important events in her life and in the life of Jesus.

**Faith Word**

**liturgical year** see p. 258

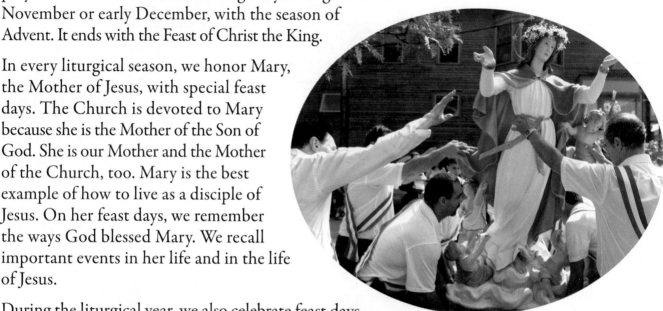

During the liturgical year, we also celebrate feast days of the saints. Saints are women, men, and children who lived lives of holiness on earth. They now share eternal life with God in heaven. The saints were faithful followers of Christ. They loved and cared for others, as Jesus did. Some of the saints even died for their belief in Christ. We learn about the saints' lives and ask them to pray with us to God.

## Activity

Create a mind map of some of the blessings, sacramentals, and devotions you have experienced. Circle the ones that were the most meaningful to you. Plan to do one of them this week.

devotions

## The Church's liturgy celebrates Christ's work of salvation.

If one of the Apostles came to your church, do you think he would recognize the Mass? After all, it's been more than two thousand years since the early Church first celebrated the mystery of Christ's Death and Resurrection in the liturgy. Our churches look very different from the first, hidden meeting places of the Apostles and their followers. We still celebrate the same mystery in the liturgy that was celebrated at the Last Supper.

Jesus' first followers might not recognize our technology, but they would recognize the Church's liturgy today. When we celebrate the Eucharist, the sacraments, and the Liturgy of the Hours, it is the same prayer all over the world.

Within the Church, we have various rituals, or ways of celebrating the liturgy. Rituals help us to understand what we celebrate and believe through prayers, gestures, and actions. Whenever Catholics celebrate and pray according to the liturgy, we all form the Church and the Body of Christ. We are joined together in some important ways:

- We share the same beliefs. We state these beliefs in our creeds, such as the Apostles' Creed.

- What the Apostles saw, heard, and experienced while they were with Jesus is the beginning of our Sacred Tradition.

- We all celebrate the Seven Sacraments.

- With our bishops, we are all united with the pope as one Church.

- We are all Catholics, who live as disciples of Jesus.

**Latin Rite matrimony celebration**

**Eastern Rite matrimony celebration**

## One Church, Many Cultures

The liturgy is celebrated in many languages and sometimes in different rituals. Our Church is catholic, which means it is universal. Most Catholics in the United States celebrate the liturgy of the Latin Church. Other Catholics celebrate the liturgy of the Eastern Church. These include Byzantine, Coptic, Syrian, Greek, and many other Churches. Each person from each nation and each culture, race, nationality, and background brings his or her own gift of self to the liturgy. When we respect these unique gifts, the Church shows welcome and appreciation to all.

## Faith Word

**devotions** see p. 257

## Blessings and devotions help us praise and thank God.

You may have seen several images of Jesus in your church. Three of these images might show Jesus falling under the weight of the Cross. These images help us to know that Jesus understands our pain. He felt physical pain and the pain of being rejected. As you sit in church and look at these images of Jesus, you can see Jesus' pain and sorrow and know that he understands when you feel sad or are hurting.

The Stations of the Cross is a **devotion** many Catholics pray and follow, especially during the season of Lent. We follow Jesus in prayer through his suffering and Death on the Cross. The Church offers many devotions to help us grow in our faith. They don't replace going to Mass and receiving the sacraments, but they can strengthen our faith.

You might pray the Rosary, alone or with your family. You might go on a pilgrimage, which is a trip to a holy site. You might take part in a feast in honor of Mary or the saints. Through personal prayer sparked by devotions, the Holy Spirit works in each of us, helping us grow in our faith and love for God.

## Partners in Faith

### Saint Cecilia

Saint Cecilia is the patron saint of musicians. When she got married, she "sang in her heart" and her husband became a Christian, too. They lived in Rome when the emperor persecuted Christians. She and her husband were both killed for their faith.

 **Learn more about the life of Saint Cecilia.**

**Faith Words**

liturgical year          devotions

## ☑ Show What You Know

Read the statements. Circle whether the statement is True or False.
Correct any false statements you find.

**1.** Rituals are the ways that we celebrate and pray the liturgy.

True / False

_____

_____

**2.** The liturgical year begins in January, the same time as the calendar year.

True / False

_____

_____

**3.** Devotions are traditions, outside of the liturgy, that help us pray and grow in faith.

True / False

_____

_____

## Live Your Faith

• During the liturgical year, we celebrate feast days of Mary, the Mother of
God, as well as the saints. In what ways do Mary and the saints show you
how to live as a follower of Jesus?

_____

_____

_____

• What can you do to honor Sunday as the Lord's Day?

_____

_____

_____

_____

## Mini-Task

While we give God thanks and praise at Mass each week, it is also important to thank God for the daily blessings in our lives. When we are thankful to someone, we can show gratitude. To show gratitude is to be thankful for something or to someone.

Turn to and talk with a partner. In what ways can expressing gratitude make you feel happy or be healthy?

The psalms are songs or prayers that often give thanks to God.

Complete your own personal Psalm of Thanksgiving.

### A Psalm of Thanksgiving

By _____ (your name here)

Shout joyfully to the Lord.

Give thanks to him, bless his name, God indeed is the Lord!

I give thanks for _____, _____,

and _____.

Know that the Lord is God, . . . we are his people.

God's mercy endures forever.

 **Want to do more? Go to your Portfolio to continue this activity.**

 At Home

Jesus celebrated with family and friends at the wedding at Cana. When we go to Mass, we celebrate with Jesus, too. The next time you're at Mass with Jesus, family, and friends, what blessings will you celebrate?

# How do we become members of the Church?

When we become part of the Church at Baptism, we become incorporated into our Lord Jesus Christ. In the Sacraments of Initiation, Jesus welcomes us into the Body of Christ. A sign is placed on our souls that can never be erased. It marks us as children of our loving Father. We are strengthened to live as Jesus' disciples.

**Go to the digital portal for a prayer of praise.**

*"Give them the spirit of wisdom and understanding, the spirit of counsel and fortitude, the spirit of knowledge and piety . . ."*

Order of Confirmation, 25

## The Sacraments of Christian Initiation join us to Christ and his Church.

When Jesus called his first disciples to join him in his mission, they followed him right away.

"As he passed by the Sea of Galilee, he saw Simon and his brother Andrew casting their nets into the sea; they were fishermen. Jesus said to them, 'Come after me, and I will make you fishers of men.' Then they abandoned their nets and followed him" (Mark 1:16–18).

**When have I felt God's love and grace?**

What made the Apostles drop everything and follow Jesus? The Holy Spirit inspired them. In a similar way, we become members of the Church by the work of the Holy Spirit in our hearts. We are joined to the Church and we are strengthened in our faith through three sacraments called the Sacraments of Christian Initiation. *Initiation* is another word for "beginning."

**The Sacraments of Christian Initiation**

- In the Sacrament of Baptism, we are joined to Jesus and the Church. A new life of grace begins in us. In Baptism, the Church welcomes us.

- In the Sacrament of Confirmation, the Holy Spirit gives us strength and courage to live as disciples of Jesus. We are sealed with the Gift of the Holy Spirit.

- The Sacrament of the Eucharist incorporates us into the Body of Christ. We are strengthened by Jesus' Body and Blood, which we receive under the appearance of bread and wine.

## Did You Know?

 **The Ring of the Fisherman is part of the pope's official attire.**

## Activity

The Sacrament of the Eucharist is at the heart of our life. In the heart shape below, write the reasons that the Eucharist is important to you. Pick one reason and share it with a partner.

**The Sacrament of Baptism forgives sin and gives us new life in Christ.**

Baptism is the sacrament in which we are welcomed into the Church. It is the first sacrament we receive. We are usually baptized as babies. In Baptism, a family might gather around the baptismal font in their church. A parent or godparent might hold the baby during the questions, Scripture readings, and special prayers.

Ordinarily the priest or deacon will gently pour water from the font over the baby's head three times while saying: "I baptize you in the name of the Father, and of the Son, and of the Holy Spirit" (*Rite of Baptism*, 60). The priest or deacon will trace the Sign of the Cross with holy oil called **chrism** on the crown of the baby's head as he prays for God's blessing on the baby.

Through the **Sacrament of Baptism**, the baby has become a member of the Church. The baby has been dressed in a white garment as a symbol of purity. This is also a sign of our new life as followers of Christ. We are given a share in the life of the Blessed Trinity.

We celebrate the Sacrament of Baptism only once. Baptism frees us from Original Sin, makes us sharers in God's own life, makes us members of the Body of Christ, and makes us temples of the Holy Spirit. All of our own sins are forgiven. Baptism also places a permanent seal, or character, on our soul, which marks us as children of God. This seal is from the Holy Spirit. It will last forever, to show that we belong to Christ forever.

## Faith Words

**chrism** see p. 257

**Baptism** see p. 257

## What Makes Us Catholic?

The holy oil used in the sacraments is so important to the Church that we celebrate a special Mass for it. At the Chrism Mass, the oil is blessed by the bishop for use all year long in Baptism, Confirmation, and Anointing of the Sick. The bishop celebrates the Mass and blesses the oil. The priests of his diocese celebrate with him and the assembly. Many dioceses celebrate the Chrism Mass on Holy Thursday or at another time during Holy Week.

**The Sacrament of Confirmation seals us with the Gift of the Holy Spirit.**

**Faith Word**

**Confirmation** see p. 257

The **Sacrament of Confirmation** deepens the grace we receive in Baptism. At Confirmation, we receive the Gift of the Holy Spirit. Confirmation deepens our spirit of adoption by God, brings us closer to Christ, and gives us strength to make the right choices. We are reminded of a time when Jesus visited the disciples after his Resurrection.

"Jesus came and stood in their midst and said to them, 'Peace be with you.' When he had said this, he showed them his hands and his side. The disciples rejoiced when they saw the Lord. [Jesus] said to them again, 'Peace be with you. As the Father has sent me, so I send you.' And when he had said this, he breathed on them and said to them, 'Receive the holy Spirit'" (John 20:19–22).

## One Church, Many Cultures

**I**n the Latin, or Roman, Catholic Church, the bishop is called the original minister of Confirmation, and the celebration of Confirmation usually occurs several years after Baptism. During the anointing of the candidate for Confirmation, the bishop uses oil that is blessed by the bishop of the diocese. In the Eastern Catholic Church, Baptism and Confirmation are celebrated at the same time, to show how these two sacraments are closely linked. The priest who baptizes also confirms.

In the Roman Catholic Church, when we receive the Sacrament of Confirmation, we are anointed with chrism, just as we were at Baptism. The bishop or priest speaks our Confirmation name and says:

BE SEALED WITH THE GIFT OF THE HOLY SPIRIT.

Then the bishop repeats Jesus' own words: "Peace be with you." We respond: "And with your spirit" (*Order of Confirmation*, 27).

Sponsors help us prepare to receive the Sacrament of Confirmation. Sponsors are Catholics who act as role models to help those who are preparing for Confirmation. Sponsors help them to grow closer to Christ.

A person preparing to receive the Sacrament of Confirmation is called a **candidate**. With the help of their sponsors, catechists, and the whole parish community, candidates learn about the mission of the Church. They pray and reflect on ways they can follow Jesus.

In the Sacrament of Confirmation, our souls are imprinted with a spiritual seal, or character, that lasts forever. Because of this, we are confirmed only once. Our anointing with oil shows that we are set apart to do God's work. We are strengthened to be disciples of Jesus. The Holy Spirit gives us the following gifts: wisdom, understanding, counsel, fortitude, knowledge, piety, and fear of the Lord. These help us to:

- love God and others, as Jesus taught
- worship God and celebrate the sacraments

**Faith Word**

candidate see p. 257

- treat others with respect
- care for the poor, hungry, and sick
- be fair
- be peacemakers
- be happy for all the gifts God has given us
- live out our faith
- stand up for what we believe.

## Activity

Compare and contrast the sacraments of Baptism and Confirmation. Add your own similarities and differences.

|  | Baptism | Confirmation |
|---|---|---|
| **Who receives it** |  |  |
| **Who administers it** |  |  |
| **What happens during the ceremony** |  |  |
| **Other people involved** |  |  |

Tell a partner which sacraments you have either celebrated or witnessed.

**The Sacrament of the Eucharist is the heart of the Church's life.**

The **Sacrament of the Eucharist** is the sacrament of the Body and Blood of Christ. Jesus gave us the Eucharist at the Last Supper:

"Then he took the bread, said the blessing, broke it, and gave it to them, saying, 'This is my body, which will be given for you; do this in memory of me.' And likewise the cup after they had eaten, saying, 'This cup is the new covenant in my blood, which will be shed for you'" (Luke 22:19–20).

In the Eucharist, Jesus pours out his grace and love for us. By the power of the Holy Spirit, Christ's suffering, Death, Resurrection, and Ascension are made present to us. The Risen Jesus is truly present—Body, Blood, soul, and divinity—under the appearance of bread and wine. When we receive Holy Communion, Jesus lives in us, and we live in him.

This is why the Sacrament of the Eucharist, which we celebrate at Mass, is at the heart of our life as Catholics. If we are aware of any mortal sins we have committed, we must first accept the **Sacrament of Penance and Reconciliation**.

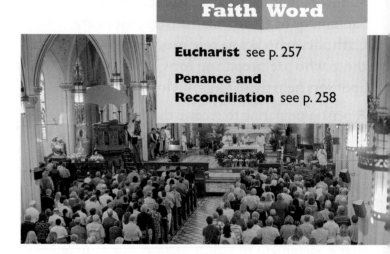

**Faith Word**

**Eucharist** see p. 257

**Penance and Reconciliation** see p. 258

Then, when we receive the Sacrament of the Eucharist, we can fully receive its life-giving effects:

- We are nourished by the Word of God and receive Jesus Christ in Holy Communion.
- We are joined more closely to Christ and one another.
- The grace we received in Baptism increases in us.
- We receive forgiveness of venial sins and strength to avoid sin.
- We are called to love and serve others, especially those in need.

## Partners in Faith

### Saint Josephine Bakhita

Saint Josephine Bakhita was a slave. She was mistreated by a few of her owners. Finally, she was given to a new master who took her to Italy. She learned about Jesus when she lived with nuns. Josephine refused to go back into slavery. She was baptized, confirmed, and received her first Communion on the same day.

 **Learn more about the life of Saint Josephine Bakhita.**

## Faith Words

chrism     Baptism     Confirmation

Penance and Reconciliation

candidate     Eucharist

 ## Show What You Know

Complete the sentences.

**1.** Baptism, Confirmation, and Eucharist are the Sacraments of Christian

_____.

**2.** In the Sacrament of the _____, we receive
the Body and Blood of Christ at Mass.

**3.** The holy oil, blessed by a bishop, that is used as a sign of the Holy Spirit

is called _____.

**4.** _____ is the sacrament that first joins us
to Christ and his Church.

**5.** A person preparing to receive the Sacrament of Confirmation is called

a _____.

## Live Your Faith

• What does it mean to you to be joined to the whole Church?

_____

_____

_____

_____

• Baptism makes us children of God. In what ways do you show others that
you are God's child?

_____

_____

_____

_____

## Mini-Task

Through the Sacraments of Initiation, we are welcomed into the Church as members of the Body of Christ. All of God's children are welcome.

What does it mean to welcome someone?

A welcome letter is a message to a new member.

In the space below, think of what you might include in a welcome letter that your parish could give to new members.

_____

_____

_____

_____

_____

_____

_____

_____

_____

_____

**Want to do more? Go to your Portfolio to continue this activity.**

# At Home

The Apostles responded to Jesus' call and lived in community, much like a family. The next time you go to Mass together, listen to the Bible readings carefully to hear Jesus' call to your family that day.

# How do we celebrate God's forgiveness and healing?

No one feels like celebrating all of the time. Sometimes we are sick. Sometimes we feel bad because we have done wrong. At times like this, Jesus wants us to draw close to him. He has given us the Sacraments of Healing to restore us and give us peace, comfort, and courage.

**Go to the digital portal for a prayer of petition.**

*"God never tires of forgiving us."*
Pope Francis, Angelus, March 17, 2013

## We receive Christ's forgiveness and healing in the Sacrament of Penance and Reconciliation.

We are meant to follow God. But sometimes we turn away from him. We become lost. Here is how Jesus brought a rich man named Zacchaeus back to God:

"[Jesus] came to Jericho and intended to pass through the town. Now a man there named Zacchaeus, who was a chief tax collector and also a wealthy man, was seeking to see who Jesus was; but he could not see him because of the crowd, for he was short in stature. So he ran ahead and climbed a sycamore tree in order to see Jesus, who was about to pass that way. When he reached the place, Jesus looked up and said to him, 'Zacchaeus, come down quickly, for today I must stay at your house.' And he came down quickly and received him with joy. When they all saw this, they began to grumble, saying, 'He has gone to stay at the house of a sinner.' But Zacchaeus stood there and said to the Lord, 'Behold, half of my possessions, Lord, I shall give to the poor, and if I have extorted anything from anyone I shall repay it four times over.' And Jesus said to him, 'Today salvation has come to this house. . . . For the Son of Man has come to seek and to save what was lost'" (Luke 19:1–10).

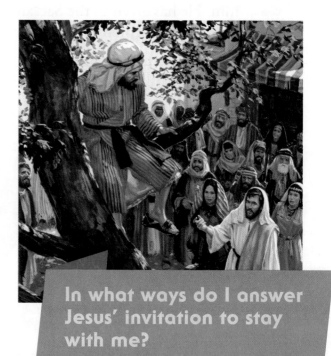

In what ways do I answer Jesus' invitation to stay with me?

## Did You Know?

**God's mercy is endless.**

## Activity

Create a storyboard retelling the story of Zacchaeus by putting the events of the story in the correct order and drawing illustrations in the boxes. Write what was said in the story in speech bubbles. Share your work with your group.

- Jesus came to Jericho.
- Jesus had dinner with Zacchaeus.
- Jesus told Zacchaeus that salvation had come to his house.
- Zacchaeus came down from the tree.
- Zacchaeus climbed a tree to see Jesus.
- Zacchaeus gave half his possessions to the poor.

In Jesus' time, tax collectors often took money for themselves when they collected taxes from people. We can tell from the story that Zacchaeus was probably guilty of this. But once he saw Jesus and spoke to him, Zacchaeus had a change of heart. He promised to return any money he had taken from people and return it four times over! This change of heart is called **conversion**. We are sorry for what we have done and, with God's grace, we will work hard not to sin again. This is known as **repentance**.

When we turn away from sin and toward God, our lives change. We live the life God wants for us. Jesus wants this for us, too. He has given us the Sacrament of Penance and Reconciliation so that our sins can be forgiven and we can receive God's grace. We can trust in God's **mercy**. Mercy is kindness and compassion shown to someone who has offended or hurt us. Here is what happens in the Sacrament of Penance and Reconciliation:

## Faith Words

conversion  see p. 257

repentance  see p. 258

mercy  see p. 258

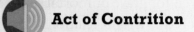

**Act of Contrition**

- We think about what we have done wrong. We express our sorrow for our sins. This is called *contrition*, or *repentance*.

- We tell all of our sins to the priest. This is called confession.

- The priest gives us *absolution*. This means God forgives us through the words and actions of the priest, who acts on Christ's behalf.

- We show that we are willing to do better. The priest gives us a *penance*. This is a prayer or an action we do after we receive absolution.

## One Church, Many Cultures

**M**any Catholics celebrate a Divine Mercy devotion first brought to the United States from the Catholic community in Poland. Saint Faustina lived in Poland and was a sister of the Congregation of Sisters of Our Lady of Mercy. She wrote about the messages she received directly from Christ, about God's Divine Mercy. Her writings began a worldwide movement of devotion to Jesus and the Eucharist as a sacrament of mercy. Every year, Latino Catholics from all over the world take part in a special devotional celebration called Encuentro Latino at the National Shrine of Divine Mercy in Massachusetts. The Church celebrates Divine Mercy Sunday on the second Sunday of Easter.

## God forgives us when we are sorry.

In the Sacrament of Penance and Reconciliation, we confess our sins directly to God through the priest who acts in the place of Christ, the eternal priest. We tell the priest the thoughts, words, and actions that have led us away from God. We should confess all of the sins we can remember and confess any mortal sins. **Mortal sins** are serious sins that sever our relationship with God and the Church. Only through the Sacrament of Penance and Reconciliation can we be forgiven for grave or mortal sins and restored to a right relationship with God.

When we receive our penance, we should do it as quickly as possible. We probably won't be asked to give half of our possessions to the poor, as Zacchaeus did. But accepting our penance shows we are willing to heal any harm we have done by our sins.

Celebrating the Sacrament of Penance and Reconciliation strengthens our friendship with God. Because we have received absolution, we are able to let go of whatever might be keeping us from loving God.

**Faith Word**

**mortal sin** see p. 258

## Activity

When we go to Confession, the priest gives us a penance. Sometimes the priest might ask you what you think would be a good penance. List what you think would be a good penance for each of the following.

Cheating on a test: _____

Disobeying a parent: _____

Stealing something: _____

Using God's name disrespectfully: _____

## Conversion and repentance are movements back to God.

When Jesus forgave sinners, he often invited them to share a meal with him, the way he did with Zacchaeus. Some people didn't think this was a good idea, and they complained to Jesus. So Jesus told them this parable:

"What man among you having a hundred sheep and losing one of them would not leave the ninety-nine in the desert and go after the lost one until he finds it? And when he does find it, he sets it on his shoulders with great joy and, upon his arrival home, he calls together his friends and neighbors and says to them, 'Rejoice with me because I have found my lost sheep.' I tell you, in just the same way there will be more joy in heaven over one sinner who repents than over ninety-nine righteous people who have no need of repentance" (Luke 15:4–7).

Jesus wants us to know that coming back into God's friendship is a good reason to celebrate. When we confess our sins, the priest is acting on behalf of Jesus. He is the sign of Jesus, the Good Shepherd, who seeks every one of his lost sheep. Jesus always seeks to bring us back to his love and peace.

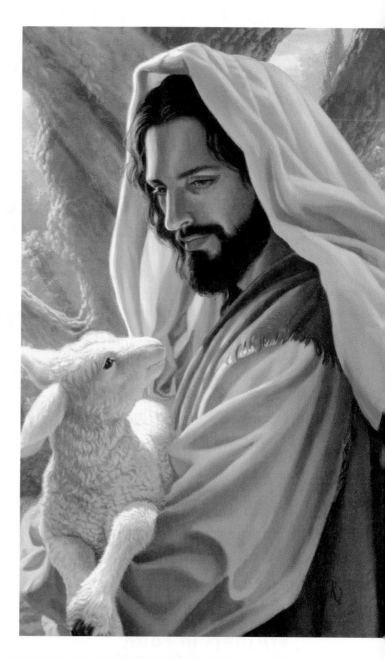

## What Makes Us Catholic?

Our sins hurt the whole Church community. Because of this, we often receive a penance for them when we celebrate the Sacrament of Penance and Reconciliation. Our penance is a sign that we are willing to repair the hurt we have caused. They show that we are able to not just say we are sorry, but also do something to make things better, or right. By doing our penance, we complete our experience of the Sacrament of Penance and receive Jesus' healing, comfort, and peace.

## The Sacrament of Anointing of the Sick continues Jesus' healing work.

When people are sick, they can become sad, anxious, or worried. They need the special help of God's grace to stay strong and keep their faith alive. They need peace and comfort. In the **Sacrament of Anointing of the Sick**, Christ shows that through his own suffering on the Cross, he understands and shares the pain of those who are seriously ill. He comforts them with his grace and gives them peace.

Like all sacraments, Anointing of the Sick is a celebration of the whole community of the Church. But most of the time, it is celebrated outside of church, in hospitals, homes, at the site of an accident, or wherever it is needed. The sacrament is meant for anyone who is seriously ill or advanced in age. It is also meant for people who are about to have surgery.

In the Sacrament of Anointing of the Sick, the priest lays his hands on the sick person, remembering that Jesus often healed the sick by laying his hands on them or simply by touching

### Faith Word

**Anointing of the Sick**
see p. 257

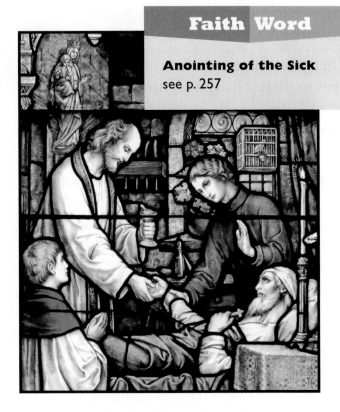

them. The priest's laying on of hands is a sign of blessing and a calling of the Holy Spirit. He anoints the person with holy oil. This is a sign of the power and presence of the Holy Spirit. It is also a sign of healing and strengthening. This sacrament continues Jesus' saving work of healing and bringing us his peace.

## Partners in Faith

### Saint Leopold Mandic

Saint Leopold wanted to be a missionary, but he wasn't healthy enough. He lived in Italy most of his life. As a priest, he spent many hours daily hearing confessions. He heard so many confessions, he is called an Apostle of Confession. He wanted people to know that God loves all of us.

 **Learn more about the life of Saint Leopold Mandic.**

## Faith Words

| conversion | repentance | mercy |
| mortal sin | Anointing of the Sick | |

 **Show What You Know**

Complete the sentences.

**1.** God's grace and _____ are given to those who are seriously ill or suffering in the Anointing of the Sick.

**2.** _____ sins are serious sins that cut us off from our relationship with God and the Church.

**3.** In the Sacrament of Penance and Reconciliation, we

_____ our sins directly to God through the person of the priest.

Place these steps of the Sacrament of Penance and Reconciliation in the order they happen: absolution, confession, contrition, penance

**1.** _____

**2.** _____

**3.** _____

**4.** _____

## Live Your Faith

• Why did Jesus give us the Sacrament of Penance and Reconciliation?

_____

_____

• In what ways have you shown mercy to others?

_____

_____

_____

_____

_____

How can I share my life with God?

## Mini-Task

We all need someone to talk to when something is bothering us or when we have a lot on our mind. God is always ready to listen to things that weigh on our heart.

The Sacrament of Penance is one way God hears and forgives our sins.

Name other people in your life who are always ready to listen when you need them.

_____

_____

_____

_____

_____

What qualities do these people have or share that make you confide in them?

_____

_____

_____

_____

_____

**Want to do more? Go to your Portfolio to continue this activity.**

## At Home

Think about people you know who are sick or who are suffering in other ways. Ask your family members if they know others who are suffering. Together, pray for them.

# How are we strengthened for service to God and others?

God calls each of us to love and serve him by loving and serving others. We are never alone in this work, because we are part of the Body of Christ. The Holy Spirit gives us strength through the Sacraments. The Sacraments at the Service of Communion give us a special grace that helps us serve God and others.

**Go to the digital portal to pray with *Lectio* and *Visio Divina*.**

*"It is Jesus who stirs in you the desire to do something great with your lives."*
Saint John Paul II, World Youth Day, August 19, 2000

## All members of the Church share in the priesthood of Christ.

Jesus Christ has many titles. We know him as the Son of God, the Good Shepherd, the Head of the Church, the Messiah, and many other good and holy titles. Jesus is also known as the High Priest. What does this mean? In the Old Testament, a priest was someone who was set apart for service to God and offered sacrifices on behalf of the people. Priests helped people connect with God.

Jesus connects people with God because Jesus is God. He has said: "If you know me, then you will also know my Father" (John 14:7). Priests in the Old Testament also made sacrifices. Jesus, our high priest, made a perfect sacrifice of his own life to save us from sin.

By our Baptism, we share in Jesus' priesthood. Our sharing in Jesus' priesthood is known as the priesthood of the faithful. This means we show Christ to the world in our actions,

**What are the ways I serve the people of my parish?**

words, thoughts, prayers, and especially in our love for God and our neighbor. We are strengthened for this mission by the Holy Spirit in the sacraments. The Sacraments at the Service of Communion give us special graces to help us serve others. These sacraments are Holy Orders and Matrimony.

## What Makes Us Catholic?

**A**s students, we learn from our teachers. The pope, bishops, and priests take their role as teachers in the Church seriously. They form the Church's teaching office, called the Magisterium. The Magisterium interprets Sacred Scripture and Sacred Tradition for current and future members of the Church. The Magisterium is guided by the Holy Spirit to help us understand Church teachings. Some of these teachings are *infallible*, which means "free from error." When we understand what we believe as a Church, we can follow those teachings and become stronger in our faith.

## Did You Know?

**There are many ways to serve God and the Church.**

## Holy Orders is a sacrament of service.

Being part of the priesthood of the faithful is not the same as being an ordained priest. In the **Sacrament of Holy Orders**, baptized men are ordained as bishops, priests, and deacons. They serve the Church in the name and person of Christ. They take on a special mission and serve God their whole lives.

In the Sacrament of Holy Orders:

- The bishop lays hands on men he has called and says a prayer of consecration. This is an important sign of God's blessing.
- Those ordained receive God's grace to carry out their ministry to the faithful.
- A spiritual seal that can never be erased is placed on the man's soul.
- Through the priest, the Church is able to continue the mission that Jesus gave to his Apostles.

Bishops are the successors of the Apostles. A successor is someone who takes on a job or title after someone else. Bishops are called to continue the mission of the Apostles. Bishops are the official teachers, leaders, and priests of the Church.

### Faith Word

**Holy Orders** see p. 257

Priests are ordained by bishops and are called to serve us by leading, teaching, and celebrating the sacraments.

Deacons are baptized men who are not priests but are ordained by their bishops for service in the Church. Some deacons are permanent deacons. They are baptized men, often but not always married or single and who serve the Church in ways that best use their individual talents and gifts. Other men serve as transitional deacons before being ordained to the priesthood. Some deacons preach or minister to the poor, the sick, or those in prison. In a special way, deacons act as Christ the Servant to others.

## Activity

Priests and permanent deacons perform different roles in parishes. They share some tasks, but they have separate callings and separate responsibilities as well. Write some of the duties of each person in the diagram.

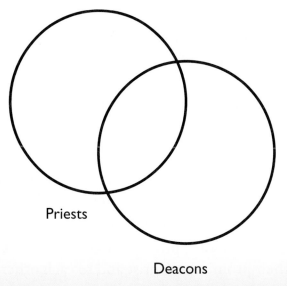

Priests

Deacons

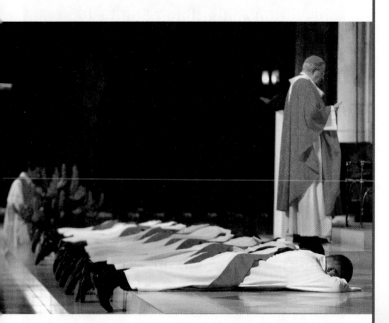

**Holy Matrimony joins a man and a woman in love with each other in Christ.**

**Faith Word**

**Matrimony** see p. 258

Jesus will always love us. He will forever keep his promise to share his life and love with us. In return, we promise to love Jesus and one another. We promise to follow and be faithful to his teachings and the teachings of the Church. This is a covenant between Jesus Christ and his Church.

When people marry, they form a covenant, too. They promise to love each other and be faithful to one another. Jesus has given us the **Sacrament of Matrimony** to bless marriages with a grace that strengthens the love and unity of the couple and helps them be open to new life. The sacrament is a sign of his love for the couple and for the Church. The sacrament is a sign of his love. The love between a husband and wife is a sign of Christ's love for his Church. That love should be generous, unselfish, faithful, honest, and true.

Jesus knows this is not easy. When Jesus turned water into wine at the wedding feast at Cana, we could see how much he cared for married couples. In the Sacrament of Matrimony, a baptized man and a baptized woman:

• promise to love and be true to each other always

• lovingly accept children as a gift from God and bring them up according to the laws of Christ and the Church

• gain the Holy Spirit's strength to live out their promise to Christ and to each other.

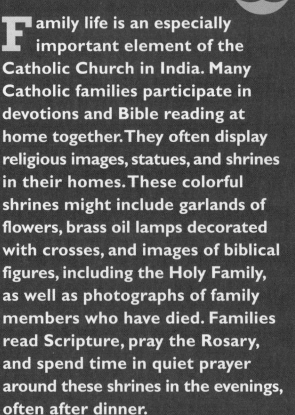

## One Church, Many Cultures

**F**amily life is an especially important element of the Catholic Church in India. Many Catholic families participate in devotions and Bible reading at home together. They often display religious images, statues, and shrines in their homes. These colorful shrines might include garlands of flowers, brass oil lamps decorated with crosses, and images of biblical figures, including the Holy Family, as well as photographs of family members who have died. Families read Scripture, pray the Rosary, and spend time in quiet prayer around these shrines in the evenings, often after dinner.

## The family is a community of grace and prayer.

When Jesus was a baby, Mary and Joseph took him to the Temple in Jerusalem.

"Now there was a man in Jerusalem whose name was Simeon. This man was righteous and devout . . . and the holy Spirit was upon him. It had been revealed to him by the holy Spirit that he should not see death before he had seen the Messiah of the Lord. He came in the Spirit into the temple; and when the parents brought in the child Jesus to perform the custom of the law in regard to him, he took him into his arms and blessed God, saying: 'Now, Master, you may let your servant go in peace, according to your word, for my eyes have seen your salvation, which you prepared in sight of all the peoples, a light for revelation to the Gentiles, and glory for your people Israel'" (Luke 2:25–32).

Jesus, Mary, and Joseph are called the Holy Family. In the Scripture account, we see that they understood how important it was to worship God in his holy place. We also see that Jesus was a light for people, even when he was a baby.

Mary, Joseph, and Jesus shared happy and sad times with their relatives and friends. They worked and prayed together. Most of all, the Holy Family honored and loved God.

## Activity

No matter how big or small it is, your family is a domestic church. Write the names of your family members on the tree. Under each person's name, write one way that you share your love with that person.

## Faith Word

**domestic church** see p. 257

Christian families are called communities of faith, hope, and love. Through our Baptism, members of every Christian family share in the very life of God the Father, Son, and Holy Spirit. This is why every Christian family is called a **domestic church**, or a "church of the home." Within our families, we learn how to cooperate and forgive. We grow in our faith and our ability to choose what is good. Our mission as Jesus' disciples begins with the people we love most. Our families give us strength to build up our neighborhoods, parishes, and nations, and even the whole world.

Your family is holy, too. It might be large or small. Your family might include parents, grandparents, brothers, sisters, aunts, uncles, and cousins. You might live with one parent or both parents. No matter what your family is like, you share your love with one another. This is a wonderful gift from God.

## Partners in Faith

### Saints Priscilla and Aquila

Saints Priscilla and Aquila were a married couple who made tents for a living. They are always mentioned together in the Bible. After they met Saint Paul, they became Christians. With Paul, they helped teach about Jesus and built churches.

 **Learn more about the lives of Saints Priscilla and Aquila.**

| **Faith** **Words** |
|---|

**Holy Orders**    **Matrimony**    **domestic church**

 **Show What You Know**

Match the terms to the correct definitions.

**Holy Orders**

**Matrimony**

**domestic church**

**deacons**

**bishops**

**priests**

the sacrament in which a man and a woman become husband and wife and promise to be faithful to each other for the rest of their lives

the sacrament in which baptized men are ordained to serve the Church as deacons, priests, and bishops

the church of the home, which every Christian family is called to be

ordained men called to serve us by leading, teaching, and celebrating the Sacraments

baptized men who are married or single and who serve the Church

the official teachers, leaders, and governors of the Church

## Live Your Faith

• In what ways can your family be a community of faith, hope, and love?

_____

_____

_____

_____

• In what ways do you show Christ to the world?

_____

_____

_____

_____

## Mini-Task

One way to follow Jesus is to serve others. Serving others is at the heart of our faith. We can and should begin to do this in our own families.

Brainstorm one way for each day of the week that you can be of service to your family.

| Sunday | |
| --- | --- |
| Monday | |
| Tuesday | |
| Wednesday | |
| Thursday | |
| Friday | |
| Saturday | |

Each day, choose one way to be of service, and complete it joyfully.

 **Want to do more? Go to your Portfolio to continue this activity.**

 # At Home

With your family, think of the deacons and priests whom you know. Do you know who the bishop of your diocese is? Say a prayer for all those who serve Jesus Christ in Holy Orders.

# Unit 3
## The Faith Lived

The Raising of Lazarus

# Unit Prayer

**Leader:** Saint Teresa of Ávila taught: "Christ has no body now on earth but yours." She prayed that we would be the hands, feet, and eyes of Christ in the world, doing good and living our faith. Let us listen to how people in the world are living their faith as the hands, feet, and eyes of Christ.

Listen to the stories of missionary disciples among us.

**Leader:** Lord Jesus, when we celebrate and give thanks for your love at Mass, we are taught how to be your Body on earth. At Communion, you give us your Body and Blood as the food we need to be your hands, feet, and eyes in the world. We are the Body of Christ.

**All:** We are the Body of Christ.

**Leader:** Christ Jesus, when people reach out to us for help, we are your hands.

**All:** We are the Body of Christ.

**Leader:** Christ Jesus, when we live our faith in the world, we are your feet.

**All:** We are the Body of Christ.

**Leader:** Christ Jesus, when we see that the world needs your love, we are your eyes.

**All:** We are the Body of Christ.

*End the Unit Prayer by singing the song for this unit.*

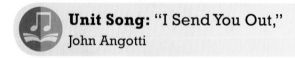

**Unit Song:** "I Send You Out," John Angotti

## Missionary Discipleship

When was someone the Body of Christ to you? What happened? How did you feel? What did you do?

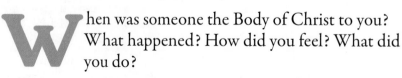

# How do we know God loves us?

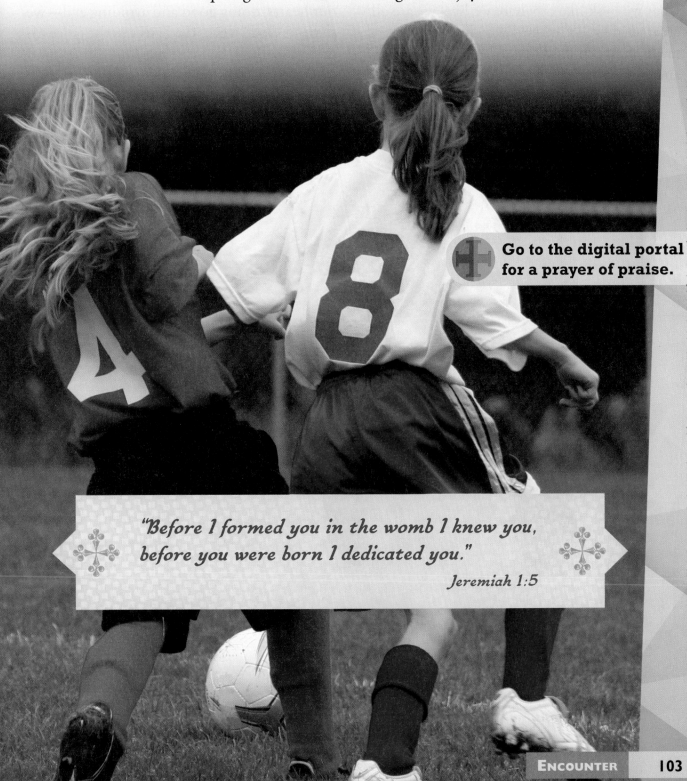

We know God loves us because he has created us in his image. He is our Father, who gives us every good gift to help us grow in his love, strength, and joy.

Go to the digital portal for a prayer of praise.

*"Before I formed you in the womb I knew you, before you were born I dedicated you."*

Jeremiah 1:5

## God created us in his own image.

God has created us in his own image. This means that, out of his total goodness, God has created you to be good, too. God has given you a body and a soul to reflect his goodness and love.

God has given each of us different abilities, languages, and backgrounds. Yet no matter what we look like or where we live, we are all created in God's image. Every human being is made to live in God's goodness and love, now and for all eternity. This is God's plan for us.

We are happiest when we live according to God's plan. We do this by sharing in his work. What is God's work? Think about what God does. He loves us. We cannot earn his love. God loves us so much that he sent his only Son, Jesus, to save us, so that we can live forever with him in peace and joy. When we love one another and ourselves the way Jesus loves us—when we follow the law God has written on our hearts, doing good and avoiding evil—we share in God's work. God gives us the grace to do this work. When you love God, others, and yourself, you are doing God's work!

How do I share in God's work?

# Did You Know?

 **There are different ways to respect.**

## Human life is sacred.

God has given each of us the ability to think, to make choices, and to love others. Of all of God's creation, only humans and angels have been given these precious gifts. Our understanding of human dignity begins with knowing that every human being is made in God's image and likeness. Each human life is sacred, at all times and in all places. We share in God's goodness, truth, and beauty, and we give him glory just by existing.

**Human dignity** is the natural value and worth each person has because we are created in God's image. Human dignity makes each of us someone, not something. It makes us all equal.

Created by God, each of us has the same **human rights**. These are the basic rights that all people have. Our most important and basic right is the right to live the life God has given us. When we take care of ourselves and others, we show respect for this right. We show our gratitude to God for his gift of life. We show that we are followers of Christ, sharing in his work.

### Faith Words

**human dignity** see p. 257

**human rights** see p. 257

### What Makes Us Catholic?

**V**alue the gift of life and respect all God's children: This is the message of the first principle of Catholic social teaching. Jesus' example of caring for those who were treated unjustly helps us to follow this important principle. The Church shows a special concern for those who are unable to speak for themselves, such as those who are unborn, elderly, or have differing abilites. This also includes those who are mistreated because of their skin color, nationality, or religion. All God's children deserve to live in justice.

### Activity

We all have the same human rights. These are basic rights that all people have. The most important right is the right to life. List some of the other basic rights all humans have.

All humans have the right to

_____.

_____.

_____.

Contribute your ideas to a class list of rights.

Respecting the dignity of others often means doing the right thing when others will not. Jesus once told a parable to show this. He said that a man had been robbed and beaten. The man was left on the road, nearly dead. Two people walked by and did nothing to help. Then a third person came along. Jesus said:

"But a Samaritan traveler who came upon him was moved with compassion at the sight. He approached the victim, poured oil and wine over his wounds and bandaged them. Then he lifted him up on his own animal, took him to an inn and cared for him. The next day he took out two silver coins and gave them to the innkeeper with the instruction, 'Take care of him. If you spend more than what I have given you, I shall repay you on my way back'" (Luke 10:33–35).

Some people did not get along with Samaritans. But in this parable, a Samaritan chose to ignore those differences.

He only knew that he had to help the stranger. He used the gifts God had given him to make a good choice. Jesus was showing us how we must see each person: as a child of God. The *Catechism of the Catholic Church* teaches that we see each person as "another self" (1944). In other words, we care for others just as we care for ourselves.

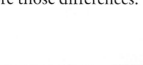

## Activity

Work in small groups to write a case study for a present-day version of the Parable of the Good Samaritan (see Luke 10:29–37). Use the following ideas to get started.

- Who might be the person who was hurt?

- What might have happened to him or her?

- Who were the people who walked by without helping?

- Who would be a Good Samaritan today?

- What could this person do to help?

## God gave us the gift of free will.

In the Parable of the Good Samaritan, two people walked past a man who needed help. They chose to do nothing. But the third person, the Samaritan, chose to help. God has given each of us the ability to choose what we will do or not do. This is called **free will**. Free will is the freedom to decide when and how to act. We use our free will when we think for ourselves and make our own decisions.

Our free will is the exercise of the freedom God has given us, but it does not mean we can say or do anything we want. We must always consider how our actions affect ourselves and

### Faith Word

**free will** see p. 257

others. We must use the gifts God has given us to make good decisions. This is how we take responsibility for our choices. We own every choice we make. Yet we are not alone when we make decisions. God gives us his help. Good decisions have a good object, a good intention, and take place in the right circumstances. When we live a life of prayer, God helps us to see more clearly how our choices affect other people and our world.

## One Church, Many Cultures

For migrants, the Catholic Church can be a place of freedom, safety, dignity, and familiar religious practices. Filipino Catholics living and working in Hong Kong have found comfort in practicing their faith together while far from home. Prayer and the sacraments give them strength while they are away from their families. New friendships are made through community gatherings. Some of these gatherings are so large that the streets around them are blocked. For Filipino Catholics, their fellow church members are a "family" with whom they can worship, share stories of challenges, and celebrate.

## Faith Words

**moral law** see p. 258

**reason** see p. 258

## The natural law is a gift from God.

The natural law is part of the **moral law**, which is the law governing all of creation according to God's justice and truth. The moral law includes the eternal law, which is the pattern of reason in the mind of God. It also includes revealed law, which is what God has taught us about what is right and wrong, good and evil, through Scripture and Tradition. Finally, the moral law includes the natural law.

The natural law is part of our very nature as creatures with **reason**. It expresses the dignity of the human person. We are created with reason. Reason helps us understand the world and know what is morally right and wrong.

The natural law is unchanging. The truths that God revealed are always true. We must obey them just as people thousands of years ago did. All people are born with reason and the natural law written on their hearts.

Our conscience is the voice of reason by which we examine our actions and judge if they are truly good or evil. We have a duty to inform our conscience. A well-formed conscience means that we can make good moral choices. We must obey our conscience and choose what is good. Spending time in prayer, reading the Bible, and participating in the sacraments will help us form our conscience properly.

Our reason is guided by natural law. Natural law does not mean that all people know what is right and wrong all the time. However, we are able to learn what is right and wrong. We learn this from God's revelation and with the help of grace.

## Partners in Faith

### Saint Joseph of Cupertino

Saint Joseph of Cupertino knew that he was made in God's image. He wanted to become a priest. He spent much time in prayer. People recognized his holiness, and many came to see him pray.

 **Learn more about the life of Saint Joseph of Cupertino.**

## Faith Words

**human dignity**     **human rights**

**free will**     **reason**     **moral law**

 **Show What You Know**

Match the terms to the correct definitions.

1. reason

2. human dignity

3. moral law

4. free will

5. human rights

the natural value and worth each person has as a result of being created in God's image

the basic rights that all people have

the freedom to decide when and how to act

the ability to think, understand, and make judgments

God's wisdom within each person that helps us know what is right and wrong

## Live Your Faith

• In what ways do you use your free will?

_____

_____

_____

_____

_____

_____

_____

• In what ways can you show you believe in human dignity?

_____

_____

_____

_____

_____

_____

_____

## Mini-Task

Each person is special. Each person was created in the image and likeness of God. Remind a friend how much God loves him or her by discovering more about him or her. Interview your friend. Ask these questions:

**1.** What is something you like to do for fun?

**2.** What is something you think no one knows about you that you would like to share?

**3.** Who is someone who has been a role model for you and your faith?

Take what you have learned about your friend and make a profile like the one shown here for him or her.

Name _____  Age _____  | Photo |

Hobbies _____

Name of school _____

Thank your friend for sharing with you.

**Want to do more? Go to your Portfolio to continue this activity.**

## At Home

In what ways can your family uphold the human dignity of one another? Of others? Plan a "Human Dignity Week." Invite your family to decide on one action the family can do this week to celebrate and respect the dignity of each family member and others in your community.

# How do we respond to God's love?

God's love is a blessing and a gift. Nothing pleases God more than when we use the many gifts he has given us. When we use God's gifts to live and make choices to serve him and others, we can live in happiness and peace, now and forever.

Go to the digital portal for a meditation prayer.

*"Whenever our interior life becomes caught up in its own interests and concerns, there is no longer room for others, no place for the poor. God's voice is no longer heard, the quiet joy of his love is no longer felt."*

Pope Francis, Evangelii Gaudium

## God has placed the desire for happiness in our hearts.

We all have days when we're happy and days when we're sad. Jesus shows us a way to live so that we can be happy now and forever. The **Beatitudes** are Jesus' teachings that describe the way God wants us to live every day.

In the Beatitudes, the word *blessed* means "happy." The Beatitudes remind us about what makes us truly happy. When we follow Jesus, we are blessed with his grace. We live a new life in the Spirit. We make the right choices that lead us to happiness now and forever.

When we follow the Beatitudes, Jesus has a message for us: "Rejoice and be glad, for your reward will be great in heaven" (Matthew 5:12).

### Faith Word

**Beatitudes** see p. 257

How am I happy even on a bad day?

 **Beatitudes**

## One Church, Many Cultures

A popular pilgrimage spot for Catholics in Israel is the Church of the Beatitudes, near the Sea of Galilee. The church stands on the top of a hill said to be near where Jesus gave the Sermon on the Mount. The building is an octagon, and its eight sides represent the eight Beatitudes Jesus gave his followers. Around the altar are mosaic tiles with symbols for the virtues. Saint John Paul II celebrated Mass at this church during his visit to the Holy Land in 2000.

## Did You Know?

 **Throughout the world, there are many different words for "happiness."**

## The Beatitudes

| | |
|---|---|
| "Blessed are the poor in spirit, for theirs is the kingdom of heaven" (Matthew 5:3). | We are poor in spirit when we empty our hearts of things we don't need, like hatred or greed. We "seek the love of God above all else" (*Catechism of the Catholic Church*, 1723). |
| "Blessed are they who mourn, for they will be comforted" (Matthew 5:4). | We mourn when we grieve with people being treated unfairly or suffering. We do what we can to help them. |
| "Blessed are the meek, for they will inherit the land" (Matthew 5:5). | We are meek when we allow God to lead us in his ways of love, kindness, and respect for all. |
| "Blessed are they who hunger and thirst for righteousness, for they will be satisfied" (Matthew 5:6). | We hunger and thirst for righteousness when we seek justice and fairness for all people. |
| "Blessed are the merciful, for they will be shown mercy" (Matthew 5:7). | We are merciful when we forgive and do not seek revenge. |
| "Blessed are the clean of heart, for they will see God" (Matthew 5:8). | We are clean of heart when we do good out of love for God and others, and not just to impress others. |
| "Blessed are the peacemakers, for they will be called children of God" (Matthew 5:9). | We are peacemakers when we listen to others and treat them with respect. |
| "Blessed are they who are persecuted for the sake of righteousness, for theirs is the kingdom of heaven" (Matthew 5:10). | We are persecuted for righteousness when others try to keep us from living as disciples of Jesus or seek to harm us for our faith. |

## Activity

Look at the chart of the Beatitudes above. Write a one-word summary for each to help you remember them.

1. _____   3. _____   5. _____   7. _____

2. _____   4. _____   6. _____   8. _____

Choose one Beatitude to practice this week. Tell a friend which one you will practice.

**Our conscience helps us to judge whether an act is right or wrong.**

The Beatitudes help guide us in the right way to live. But when it's time to make choices, how can we know what to do? God has given us a **conscience** to help us. Our conscience helps us know the difference between right and wrong, between good and evil. Whenever we make a decision, our conscience helps us answer three important questions:

**Faith Word**

conscience  see p. 257

- **What are our choices?** Our conscience helps us see our choices in light of what we already know is good and evil, right and wrong.

- **What is involved?** Sometimes a decision that seems good is actually not good in light of the circumstances, or what is happening around us. For example, playing is usually a good thing. However, choosing to play instead of doing homework is not a good decision.

- **What do we want to happen?** Our conscience helps us to know what our intentions are. Intentions are what we hope will happen as a result of something we do. For example, if we help someone because we truly want what is good for him or her, our intentions are good. But if we help someone only because we want something in return or we want a reward, these are not good intentions of kindness or love. Selfish intentions can take away from the goodness of what we do.

Some actions are always wrong for us to choose. We must never choose to do something that is wrong in order to make something good happen.

For example, it is never right to use violence to make a positive change in society. Jesus taught his disciples to speak out against injustice by preaching the Good News and by their own example of love for others.

## Activity

Make a mind map of one of the gifts of the Holy Spirt (see page 115). Write the gift in the center and fill in the other sections with words and phrases you connect to that gift.

**Faith, hope, and charity are gifts from God.**

When we live in the light of God's love, we work to make the best use of his many gifts to us. We can make doing good a habit, or a way of life. Virtues are habits of doing good. They are qualities of character, built up by repeated actions, that help us live a good life. The most important virtues come from God. They are called the **Theological Virtues**. They are faith, hope, and charity.

**Faith Words**

**Theological Virtues** see p. 259

**gifts of the Holy Spirit** see p. 257

Faith helps us believe that God is with us and acting in our lives. Yes, we choose to believe in God, but faith is also a gift. Even the freedom that lets us choose is first a gift from God.

Hope helps us put God first and keep focused on heaven as our goal. Hope helps us spread God's Kingdom on earth and look forward to the Kingdom in heaven.

Charity is the greatest of all virtues. Charity is another way to say love. We love God and our neighbor because God loves us. God's love for us never ends. He gives us the ability to love forever, too.

The Holy Spirit gives us many gifts, too. The seven **gifts of the Holy Spirit** that we receive at Baptism help us follow God's law and live as Jesus did. In the Sacrament of Confirmation, these gifts are increased in us.

## Gifts of the Holy Spirit

- **Wisdom** helps us follow God's will.

- **Understanding** helps us love and appreciate others.

- **Counsel** (right judgment) helps us make good decisions that follow God's laws.

- **Fortitude** (courage) helps us to be strong in our faith and witness to Jesus; we can stand up for what is right.

- **Knowledge** helps us learn more about God and his love for us.

- **Piety** (reverence) helps us show love and respect for God.

- **Fear of the Lord** (wonder and awe) helps us see God's presence in our lives and in the world.

## Catholic social teaching helps us to work for the common good.

Imagine getting up in the morning without a single person there. Outside, you cannot hear or see anyone. At school, there are no other students or teachers. You are completely alone.

This is not how God made us to live. We want and need to live and work with others. In the Beatitudes, Jesus shows us how much we depend on God and one another. He shows us how

### Faith Words

**common good** see p. 257

**justice** see p. 258

much God loves and cares for us. God has given each of us the responsibility of loving and caring for one another just as he does. Each of us is called to live in a way that respects all life as a gift from God. We are meant to seek the **common good**. The common good is achieved when all people in a society have an equal chance to fulfill their gifts and their unique calling by God.

In Catholic social teaching, the Church calls on all people to work together so this can happen. We seek peace and justice for everyone. **Justice** means respecting the rights of others and giving them what is rightfully theirs.

Everyone is responsible for working together to promote justice. As Catholics, we have a special responsibility to treat others as we would want to be treated, as Jesus calls us to do. We imitate Jesus by respecting people in our families, at our schools, in our neighborhoods, and all over the world. This is how we live the Beatitudes.

## What Makes Us Catholic?

The Church works for justice and peace, and it celebrates this work at Mass. The United States Conference of Catholic Bishops explains that at Mass, the readings from Sacred Scripture announce "God's reign of justice and peace." Because everything we do is meant to build God's Kingdom, Catholic social teachings are "proclaimed whenever we gather for worship."

## Partners in Faith

### Blessed Andrew of Phú Yên

The Beatitudes say that those who are persecuted will see heaven. Blessed Andrew of Phú Yên lived in Vietnam during a time of great persecution. He was beaten and put in prison, but he refused to give up his faith. His last words were to praise Jesus and encourage others.

 **Learn more about the life of Blessed Andrew of Phú Yên.**

## Faith Words

**Beatitudes**        **conscience**
**Theological Virtues**
**gifts of the Holy Spirit**
**common good**        **justice**

 **Show What You Know**

Complete the following sentences.

1. The _____ is achieved when all people in a society have the chance to fulfill their gifts and their unique calling by God.

2. God's gifts of faith, hope, and charity are known as the _____.

3. _____ means respecting the rights of others and giving them what is rightfully theirs.

4. The _____ are the teachings of Jesus that describe the way to live as his disciples.

5. The seven gifts that help us follow God's law and live as Jesus did are the

_____.

## Live Your Faith

• In what ways does your conscience help you?

_____

_____

_____

_____

• What Beatitude most helps you live as Jesus' disciple?

_____

_____

_____

_____

## Mini-Task

The Beatitudes are Jesus' guide for being happy in this world. They remind us that what matters most is not how much "stuff" we have but how we care for and respect other people.

The Beatitudes are two thousand years old, yet they still apply to our lives today.

Think about what is happening in the world today. Reread each Beatitude in the chart. Give a modern-day example of each Beatitude, based on Jesus' words.

| Beatitude | Modern-Day Example |
|---|---|
| **"Blessed are the poor in spirit, for theirs is the kingdom of heaven"** (Matthew 5:3). | |
| **"Blessed are they who mourn, for they will be comforted"** (Matthew 5:4). | |
| **"Blessed are the meek, for they will inherit the land"** (Matthew 5:5). | |
| **"Blessed are the peacemakers, for they will be called children of God"** (Matthew 5:9). | |

 **Want to do more? Go to your Portfolio to continue this activity.**

# At Home

With your family, talk about the importance of working for the good of your family. Name something each of you could do for the good of all in your family.

# How does God teach us to love?

As our loving Father, God wants all of his children to get along with one another. God has given us the Ten Commandments to show us how to love him and one another the way God loves each of us.

 **Go to the digital portal for a prayer of adoration.**

> *"Hear, O Israel! The LORD is our God, the LORD alone! Therefore, you shall love the LORD, your God, with your whole heart, and with your whole being, and with your whole strength."*
>
> *Deuteronomy 6:4–5*

## We understand God's law through Divine Revelation and human reason.

God wants to give us every possible way to know him, love him, and serve him. He has set his wisdom in our hearts. He has given us a conscience so we can know what is right and wrong. He has given us the gift of human reason so we can think about our choices. Yet God wants us to know his law as clearly as we can so we make good moral choices. That is why God gave Moses the Ten Commandments. They summed up everything God wanted to teach his people about how to live.

The Ten Commandments were written on stone tablets. God shared these laws directly with his people.

"The LORD said to Moses: This is what you will say to the Israelites: You have seen for yourselves that I have spoken to you from heaven" (Exodus 20:22).

Through the Ten Commandments, or the Old Law, God wanted to prepare people to understand even more about justice and love. In time, he sent his Son, Jesus, to help us. Jesus gave us a way to understand these laws even more deeply. We call this the New Law, or the law of love:

"I give you a new commandment: love one another. As I have loved you, so you also should love one another" (John 13:34).

 **1 Corinthians 13:4–8**

**How do I show love and care for another person?**

## Did You Know?

 **Every country has laws.**

## The Ten Commandments guide our relationship with God.

God gave us the Ten Commandments so we could know how to live a life of love. The first three commandments show us how we can put God first. When we do this, everything else in our lives falls into place. We can grow strong in God's love.

In the First Commandment, God tells us: "You shall have no other gods before me." One way we put God first is by respecting God's name and the name of Jesus. The Second Commandment says: "You shall not take the name of the LORD your God in vain." This tells us that God's name is holy. We treat it with **reverence**. *Reverence* means "honor, love, and respect." We never use God's name carelessly or in anger. We also respect the names of Mary and the saints.

We also honor God by following the Third Commandment: "Remember to keep holy the LORD's Day," Sunday. Every Sunday we gather as a community for the celebration of the Mass. Taking part in the Mass every Sunday is the most important way we can keep the Lord's Day holy. This is because the Eucharist is at the heart of our worship.

The Lord's Day is also a day for rest and relaxation. There are many ways we can honor God. We can gather with people we love and care for. This strengthens our families and friendships. We can share the gifts God has given us to help others. We can spend time reading the Bible or stories of saints to help us grow closer to God. We can refrain from doing unnecessary work.

### Faith Word

reverence see p. 259

 **Ten Commandments**

## One Church, Many Cultures

**W**hile Catholics name Sunday as the Lord's Day, Mass is celebrated all throughout the week in most countries. In some cultures, the day of "rest" is defined by government work schedules or practices of major religions other than Christianity. Even in the United States, some jobs require people to be at work on Sundays or Saturday evenings. The time we take with our families at church and at home on our day of rest strengthens and refreshes us for the week ahead.

## The Ten Commandments guide our relationships with others.

Each of the Ten Commandments is a guide for living a moral life. The Fourth through Tenth Commandments show how we should love and care for ourselves and others.

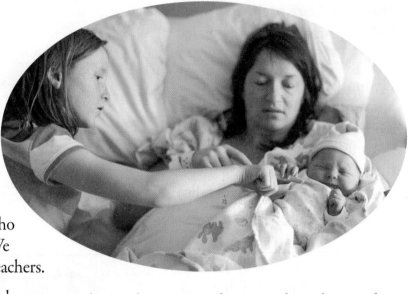

The Fourth Commandment is: "Honor your father and your mother." This means honoring our parents and those who take care of us. We owe them respect. We respect people in authority, such as our teachers.

The Fifth Commandment is based on the natural moral truth that all life is sacred, created by God: "You shall not kill." To follow this commandment, we value and respect life in all its forms. We do nothing to harm any person. We do not hate others or seek revenge. We take care of ourselves and those in need in our homes, neighborhoods, country, and world. We promote peace.

The Sixth Commandment is about love and the way we show our love: "You shall not commit adultery." We are called to honor the love that a husband and wife have for each other. We honor their promise to be faithful. From this commandment, we learn that we must honor all of our promises and respect our creation as male and female as a gift from God.

## What Makes Us Catholic?

**Y**ou may often see a plaque or other display of the commandments in church. The Ten Commandments express the natural moral law and are the foundation for many laws and codes developed throughout history, including in the United States. They are also the foundation for some of the laws we are given as part of our responsibilities as members of the Church. You will learn more about these laws, called the Precepts of the Church, on page 124.

## Activity

"Hear, O Israel! The LORD is our God, the LORD alone!" (Deuteronomy 6:4).

This Bible verse is called the *Shema*, and the Jewish people still pray it. Jesus would have prayed it, too. Write it below. Pray the verse together with your group.

_____

_____

_____

_____

_____

_____

_____

**Faith Word**

**covet** see p. 257

The Seventh Commandment is: "You shall not steal." This is about the ways we treat other people and the things that belong to them. It is based on justice, respecting the rights of others and giving them what is rightfully theirs. We never take what belongs to another. Justice calls us to care for all that God has created. We show respect for things that do not belong to us. We share.

The Eighth Commandment is: "You shall not bear false witness against your neighbor." This is about telling the truth. We tell the truth by avoiding all lies. We respect the privacy of others. We do not gossip or spread rumors. We apologize and make things right if we have said something that was not true.

The Ninth Commandment is: "You shall not covet your neighbor's wife." This commandment is about love and respect. We practice purity of heart, which means we are patient and decent. We practice modesty, which means that we speak and act with respect for ourselves and others.

The Tenth Commandment is: "You shall not covet your neighbor's goods." To **covet** means to wrongly desire something that

belongs to someone else. We also do not envy what others have. To envy is to be sad that someone else has good things, wishing we had them instead. We can be grateful for what we do have and trust that God has our good in mind in all things.

## Activity

The Eighth Commandment is about telling the truth. Find a partner and talk about what you would do in the following situations:

- A friend asks you to say you were with him or her when you weren't. If you tell the truth, your friend will get in big trouble.

- Your parents think your sibling broke a dish, but you broke it.

- Your teacher asks where your homework is. You haven't done it, but if you say it's in your desk, you'll have time to finish it.

Share your ideas with another pair or in small groups.

## The Precepts of the Church strengthen our union with God and the Church.

We gain strength to follow the commandments by taking part in the Mass. Here, we listen to the Word of God and understand how it can guide us in our daily lives. We can know that what we learn about the Word of God at Mass is the truth because it comes to us from the Holy Spirit. At Mass, we are strengthened by Jesus in the Eucharist. Receiving Communion once a year during the Easter season is a Precept of the Church. The **Precepts of the Church** strengthen Christian discipleship.

The Precepts of the Church (see page 252) are our responsibilities as members of the Body of Christ. We take part in the Mass. We confess our sins in the Sacrament of Penance and Reconciliation. We help to support the Church in whatever ways we are able. These are some of the ways we can grow as Jesus' disciples. They are ways we support the Church, too.

### Faith Word

**Precepts of the Church**
see p. 258

### Partners in Faith
#### Saint Louis of Toulouse

Saint Louis of Toulouse was born to a rich family. He was related to kings and queens in Europe. Despite his wealth, Saint Louis was willing to give up his fortune because he trusted that God would give him all he needed. The city of San Luis Obispo, California, is named after him.

 **Learn more about the life of Saint Louis of Toulouse.**

## Faith Words

**reverence**        **covet**

**Precepts of the Church**

 **Show What You Know**

Answer the questions.

1. What is another word for how we honor, love, and respect God?

   _____

2. What do we do when we wrongly desire something that belongs to someone else?

   _____

3. What are some rules that help us to be good Catholics?

   _____

## Live Your Faith

• In what ways do the Precepts of the Church guide you in your faith?

_____

_____

_____

_____

_____

_____

• What do you do to avoid envying or coveting what other people have?

_____

_____

_____

_____

_____

_____

## Mini-Task

The commandments remind us that our relationship with God should be at the center of our lives. In our busy world, it's easy to focus on the many things there are to do, such as school, sports, activities, and social events.

While these are all good ways to spend our time, what steps do we take to make time for God?

In the calendar entry below, write the date of this coming Sunday and design a plan for ways you will make time for God. Write down each action you will take to do so.

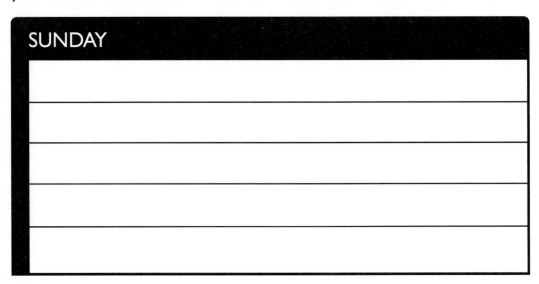

**SUNDAY**

Turn and talk to a partner. In what way will each item on your planner honor the Lord's Day?

 **Want to do more? Go to your Portfolio to continue this activity.**

##  At Home

Talk as a family about what you can do to honor the Third Commandment: Keep holy the Lord's Day.

God never stops loving us, ever. He loves us even when we choose to turn away from him. He loves us when we come to him in sorrow for our sins. He loves us as he forgives us and helps us do better. Nothing we can do can make God stop loving us.

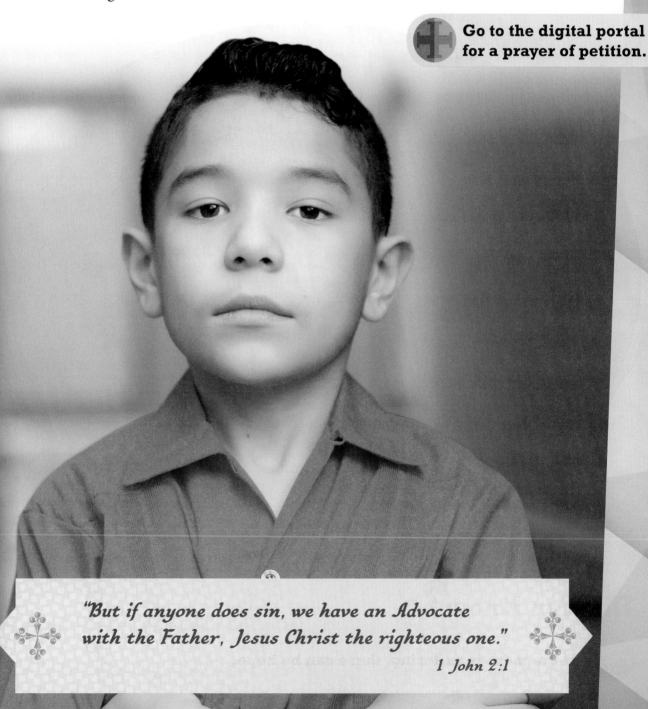

**Go to the digital portal for a prayer of petition.**

*"But if anyone does sin, we have an Advocate with the Father, Jesus Christ the righteous one."*

*1 John 2:1*

## Original Sin affects all people.

God has given us many gifts so that we can live in his happiness forever. Yet sometimes we might wonder why there is still so much unhappiness in the world. There is pain and suffering. People are often treated unfairly. Why does this happen?

In the account of Adam and Eve, we learned about Original Sin. This was the sin of the first humans, who made a choice to disobey God. In doing so, they turned away from God's loving plan of happiness for all his creatures. Sin, suffering, pain, and evil came into the world. This is the effect of Original Sin.

We are born with Original Sin, and we are affected by it all through our lives. It inclines us to choose sin. This is why God sent his Son, Jesus, to us. Through his Cross and Resurrection, Jesus saves us from sin.

How can I help someone who is suffering or hurting?

## Did You Know?

 **Where there is suffering, there can be hope.**

## Sin is a choice to turn away from God.

God has given us the gift of free will to make our own choices. When we make choices that help us know, love, and serve God, we are making good choices. Choices that turn us away from God's loving plan for us might seem easier or more fun, but they will not make us happy in the end.

We can be tempted to make bad choices. A **temptation** is an attraction to choose sin. When we are tempted to sin, we can look to Jesus as an example of what to do.

As Jesus was beginning his work, he went to the desert to pray. There, the Devil tried to tempt him. He wanted Jesus to turn away from God his Father. But Jesus trusted his Father. He told the Devil to go away. Jesus said:

"It is written: 'The Lord, your God, shall you worship and him alone shall you serve'" (Matthew 4:10).

Jesus always trusted his Father. He chose to do all his Father willed.

### Faith Word

**temptation** see p. 259

### What Makes Us Catholic?

**M**atthew 4:1–11 tells us about the temptation of Jesus in the desert. This Gospel account is sometimes read at Mass on the First Sunday of Lent. Jesus did not give in to temptation. He loved his Father and wanted to do his will. This Gospel helps us understand the power that temptation can have if we don't trust in God. When we resist temptation and follow God's plan, we share in Jesus' victory over evil.

**Faith Word**

venial sin  see p. 259

## Sin goes against God's law.

Sin is a thought, word, or action that goes against God's law. Sin hurts our relationship with our loving Father. Some sins are very serious. These are mortal sins. Mortal sin breaks our friendship with God. Those who commit mortal sin lose sanctifying grace. Yet God never stops loving them. He offers forgiveness, even for mortal sins, in the Sacrament of Penance and Reconciliation. He gives us his grace.

A less serious sin that hurts a person's friendship with God is a **venial sin**. Venial sins do not remove sanctifying grace, but they hold people back from being as good as God made them to be. Venial sin also weakens our ability to avoid mortal sin.

No matter how, when, or why we sin, we fall short of being the person God wants us to be. Every sin turns us away from God and his plan for us. It weakens our friendship with God.

### One Church, Many Cultures

At World Youth Day celebrations, everyone is invited to receive the Sacrament of Penance and Reconciliation. Often there are outdoor confessionals where young people can confess their sins to a priest. The sacrament is celebrated in several languages. There are also times for groups to gather for an examination of conscience. When we celebrate this sacrament, the whole Church receives healing. On World Youth Day in 2016, Pope Francis heard confessions.

### Activity

Some sins *break* friendships, and some sins *hurt* friendships. One way to understand the difference is to think about what might happen in a situation with your best friend.

Write one thing that could make your friend upset with you.

_____

Write one thing that could make your friend not want to be your friend anymore.

_____

Share with the group what happens when you tell a friend you are sorry and you ask for forgiveness. Share what happens when you tell *God* you are sorry and you ask for forgiveness.

## Sin harms our relationship with God.

Sometimes we might make a choice we know is wrong. We think it is very small and it didn't hurt anyone. We don't worry about it. But the sin has weakened us. The next time we are faced with a chance to sin, it can be easier to do it. But this time, it hurts us more. It might make us want to sin again, and it can make it easier for us to choose to sin. When we repeat sins, we are not living up to what God wills for us.

When we choose to sin, we choose not to trust God. We can become afraid of trusting God. If we commit venial sin again and again, it can lead to a more serious mortal sin. This is why even a venial sin can put us in danger of separating ourselves from God completely.

## Activity

God wants us to ask forgiveness every time we sin.
A good habit is to pray an Act of Contrition.
Write your own Act of Contrition, using the following terms:

**forgive**      **love**      **sin**      **sorry**      **change**

_____

_____

_____

_____

_____

Teach your prayer to a partner.

Whenever we sin, we need to seek God's help and forgiveness. When we are sorry for our sins, God is always ready to forgive us and help us try again. Even if we commit the same sin again, God is still ready to forgive us. He wants to help us avoid sin. We can ask God to forgive us every day. God knows what is in our hearts.

Sometimes we might think something we have done is not a sin, even though it is. We still need to understand why it hurts God and others. For instance, imagine you are angry at a friend for something he did to you. So you refuse to talk to your friend. You might even say something mean to your friend, which you think is okay. After all, he did something to you. This is not how Jesus wants us to live. Jesus wants us to forgive others just as his Father forgives us.

## Partners in Faith

### Saint Moses the Black

Saint Moses was often tempted to say or do mean things. Yet each time he did so, he turned away from temptation by praying. Sometimes he became discouraged because he never seemed to be good enough. A friend, Saint Isidore, told him to never give up trying.

 **Learn more about the life of Saint Moses the Black.**

## Faith Words

temptation        venial sin

 **Show What You Know**

In your own words, write definitions for the terms.

**1. mortal sin**

_____

_____

_____

_____

**2. temptation**

_____

_____

_____

_____

**3. venial sin**

_____

_____

_____

_____

## Live Your Faith

• In what ways does your faith help you avoid temptation?

_____

_____

• What actions could help you avoid committing venial sins?

_____

_____

_____

## Mini-Task

God created us to be kind and loving. He wants us to treat others as we would like to be treated. When our friends are doing something we know is wrong, it can be difficult to stand apart from the group and make another choice.

In the space below, write a prayer. Ask God to give you the courage to stand up for what you know is right and to resist the temptation to join in when others do wrong things.

**Prayer for Courage**

_____

_____

_____

_____

_____

_____

_____

_____

Teach your prayer to a partner.

 **Want to do more? Go to your Portfolio to continue this activity.**

 **At Home**

Pray the Lord's Prayer with your family. Listen to the words in the prayer about sin and temptation. Pray for the strength not to sin, and pray that your friends and family will be strong, too.

## What turns us toward God's love?

We cannot turn away from sin on our own. We need God's help. Jesus has given us the gift of his own life to save us from sin. This is the grace we receive in our Baptism. Through Jesus' gift of grace, we can turn away from sin and turn toward God our Father. We can live in true freedom in God's love.

**Go to the digital portal for a *Lectio* and *Visio Divina* prayer.**

*"The grace of our Lord Jesus Christ, and the love of God,*
*and the communion of the Holy Spirit be with you all."*

*Introductory Rites of the Mass, Roman Missal*

## God's grace helps us turn away from sin.

Jesus often spent time with crowds of people who wanted to meet him and learn from him. Bartimaeus was one of these people.

"And as [Jesus] was leaving Jericho with his disciples and a sizable crowd, Bartimaeus, a blind man, . . . sat by the roadside begging. On hearing that it was Jesus of Nazareth, he began to cry out and say, 'Jesus, son of David, have pity on me.' And many rebuked him, telling him to be silent. But he kept calling out all the more, 'Son of David, have pity on me.' Jesus stopped and said, 'Call him.' So they called the blind man, saying to him, 'Take courage; get up, he is calling you.' He threw aside his cloak, sprang up, and came to Jesus. Jesus said to him in reply, 'What do you want me to do for you?' The blind man replied to him, 'Master, I want to see.' Jesus told him, 'Go your way; your faith has saved you.' Immediately he received his sight and followed him on the way" (Mark 10:46–52).

Bartimaeus might have thought he had nothing to offer Jesus, yet Jesus healed him. He saw that Bartimaeus had gifts. More

**What does God want from me?**

important than giving Bartimaeus his sight, Jesus gave him healing and hope.

We don't have to do anything to receive God's grace. But when we accept it, we become truly free to live the life God wants us to live.

## Did You Know?

**Hope heals.**

## God's grace helps us respond to his mercy.

Jesus' followers probably thought Bartimaeus just wanted to see the world around him. But Jesus knew what was in his *heart*. He knew Bartimaeus needed the same thing that everyone else needed. Bartimaeus needed to know and love God.

Because we are created in God's image, the desire for God is deep inside us. We want to be free to be with God. But because of the effects of Original Sin, all of humanity was separated from God. This is why Jesus came: to free us from our sin and to restore our relationship to God.

Sin is what holds us back from living in God's love. Jesus' Death and Resurrection freed us from sin and death. Jesus saved us so that we can receive the grace to live in God's love. This is what **salvation** is. Our salvation comes through Jesus and his Father's merciful love for us.

**Faith Word**

salvation see p. 259

## What Makes Us Catholic?

The word *salvation* comes from *salvare*, a Latin word that means "to save." The saving work of Jesus is so important to the Church that the words *save* and *salvation* appear often in various forms in the prayers and songs of the liturgy. And we often speak of Jesus as *Savior*, one of the many titles for the Son of God. In the mystery of faith at Mass, we pray:

"Save us, Savior of the world,
for by your Cross and Resurrection
you have set us free."

We call this prayer a mystery of faith because we can never fully understand the power of Christ's saving love and mercy except through faith. We can, however, accept this gift of salvation and thank God for it.

Because of Jesus' Death and Resurrection, we can receive the gift of God's grace through the Holy Spirit. Grace is a share of God's life within us. God's life is good and holy. It is eternal life. This means that when we receive God's grace, we are sharing in God's good, holy, and eternal life right now!

Jesus told Bartimaeus that his faith had saved him. This is because Bartimaeus had responded to God's grace by having faith in Jesus. He asked Jesus for what he needed, and he believed Jesus could give it to him. Then Bartimaeus put his faith into action by following Jesus "on the way." With Jesus' healing grace, Bartimaeus was free to live the life God wanted for him. With God's grace, we can live the life of grace God has planned for us, too.

## One Church, Many Cultures

Some Catholics celebrate the grace that God gives us in spiritual groups called movements. The Focolare Movement was founded by an Italian teacher during World War II. Focolare is Italian for "family hearth," or a place to stay warm beside a fire. During the war, Chiara Lubich heard God's call for peace and love. She gathered her friends to minister to those who were suffering and afraid. Once the war ended, the Focolare Movement became a form of religious life. There are now more than five million members, many of them young people. Focolare members live and work in more than 180 countries around the world.

## Activity

In the diagram, write things that you want and need. In the outer circle, write some things you *want*. In the middle circle, write some things you both *want and need*. In the inner circle, write some things you *need*. In the center of the circle, write what you need most from God. Ask yourself: What is the difference between what I want and what I need?

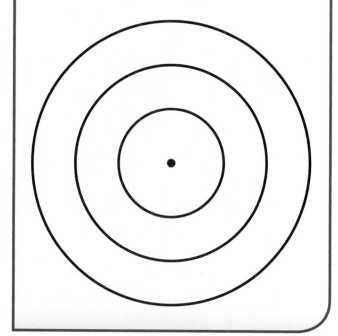

## The Holy Spirit fills our hearts with sanctifying grace.

We receive a special kind of grace in the Sacrament of Baptism called **sanctifying grace**. This grace

- allows us to share in God's life
- is strengthened by the sacraments
- is strengthened by actual grace
- leads us to eternal life.

Sanctifying grace allows us to share in God's life. Through the forgiveness of sins, sanctifying grace is restored through the Sacrament of Penance and Reconciliation. Sanctifying grace is not something we can see, touch, or hear. Yet it is more effective than anything because it is from the Holy Spirit.

### Faith Word

**sanctifying grace**
see p. 259

## Activity

God wants us to lead a life of holiness. Using the letters of the word, write an acrostic poem about the things you think of when you hear the word *holy*. Draw a star next to the one word that means the most to you right now.

H _____

O _____

L _____

Y _____

**Faith Word**

conversion see p. 257

## Moved by grace, we turn toward God and away from sin.

When we receive God's grace in our hearts, we can respond to God's call to conversion. **Conversion** means turning to God with our whole heart, turning away from sin and trusting in God. When we trust God, he will show us how we can change and grow into the people he wants us to be.

Sin weakens or breaks our relationship with God and with one another. But when we come to God in the Sacrament of Penance and Reconciliation, our friendship with God becomes stronger. The life of grace in us is restored or strengthened. Our relationship with the Church, the Body of Christ, is made stronger, too.

The grace we receive gives us the strength to live by the Ten Commandments and Jesus' teachings, especially in the Beatitudes. We find that we can truly love one another as Jesus has loved us. Grace helps us follow Jesus.

## Partners in Faith
### Saint Angela of Foligno

As a young woman, Saint Angela of Foligno was more interested in money and parties than she was in God. At about the age of 40, she had a conversion experience. She turned away from sin and began to trust God. She asked God for forgiveness. She helped the poor with her money. She even nursed the sick herself.

 **Learn more about the life of Saint Angela of Foligno.**

## Faith Words

**salvation**  **sanctifying grace**

**conversion**

 **Show What You Know**

Read the statements. Circle whether the statement is True or False.
Correct any false statements you find.

1. Conversion means turning to God in our thoughts only. True / False

   _____

   _____

2. Sanctifying grace is the gift of sharing in God's life, given in the Sacrament of Baptism
   and sometimes restored in the Sacrament of Penance. It allows us to live in friendship
   with God. True / False

   _____

   _____

3. Salvation is the restoring of friendship with God but not forgiveness
   of our sins. True / False

   _____

   _____

## Live Your Faith

• In what ways have you experienced conversion in your life?

   _____

   _____

   _____

   _____

• How can you respond to God's gift of sanctifying grace?

   _____

   _____

   _____

## How is my faith visible to others?

## Mini-Task

The Gospel account of Jesus healing Bartimaeus helps us remember that Jesus came to offer salvation to everyone, not only people who are rich or famous. It also shows us that Jesus has the power to do anything.

Imagine that the account of Bartimaeus and his encounter with Jesus is becoming a novel. Design a book jacket that would give a reader an idea of the Scripture narrative and also be eye-catching enough for a reader to pick it up.

Your jacket must include:

• a clear title

• a graphic design that reflects the themes of the novel

• a summary of the plot without giving away the ending

• a review (opinion) about the narrative

• a design that is appropriate for the intended audience of your book.

 **Want to do more? Go to your Portfolio to continue this activity.**

 **At Home**

God gives us our families to guide one another in holiness and to lead us to salvation. Talk with your family members about ways each of you can help the family grow in holiness.

How do we become what we believe?

The Pharisee and the Tax Collector

143

# Unit Prayer

**Leader:** Saint Teresa of Ávila felt that we should be happy and celebrate that we are children of God. She felt that we should see God as one who loves us because we are his children. We must all try to live as children of God. God created us in his likeness and loves us beyond our imagination.

Let us listen to how missionary disciples among us live as children of God.

**Leader:** O God and Father, we, your children, thank you for your love.

**All:** We are the children of God.

**Leader:** O God, Father of Jesus, bless us as your children to bring your love to others.

**All:** We are the children of God.

**Leader:** Loving God, we celebrate the many gifts that you have given us, and we praise your name.

**All:** We are the children of God.

**Leader:** O God, you call us each by name and have loved us as no other can love us.

**All:** We are the children of God.

*End the Unit Prayer by singing the song for this unit.*

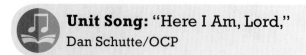

**Unit Song:** "Here I Am, Lord," Dan Schutte/OCP

## Missionary Discipleship

We are all children of God. When did you treat someone else as a child of God? What was it like?

# What is prayer?

**P**rayer is a conversation with God. God speaks to us in our hearts and we respond. In prayer, we speak to God as a Father who loves us. God is always ready to hear our prayer, and our prayer helps bring us closer to God.

**Go to the digital portal for a meditation prayer.**

*"Remember that you are never alone: Christ is with you on your journey every day of your lives! He has called you and chosen you to live in the freedom of the children of God. Turn to him in prayer and in love. . . . Walk with him who is 'the Way, the Truth, and the Life'!"*

*Saint John Paul II, World Youth Day, August 23, 1997*

## Faith Word

**prayer** see p. 258

## In prayer, we speak to God.

God has made us in his image. God calls to each of us deep in our hearts. **Prayer** is talking and listening to God and our response to his will for our lives. When we pray, we raise our hearts and minds to God. We do not have to be afraid to ask God for anything in prayer. We can speak to God about what is deepest in our hearts and on our minds.

When we were younger, we might have asked God for things only for ourselves. But as we grow, we learn to listen to what God wants for us. We begin to seek the good things God wants for us and for others.

What do I want to say to God right now?

# Did You Know?

 **Prayer can change your life.**

## In prayer, we listen to God.

God calls everyone to seek him. He calls us to love him as he loves us. In the Bible, we read that God often calls people in mysterious ways. He spoke to Moses for the first time when Moses was out tending his sheep. Moses spotted a bush that was on fire. He could see flames coming out of the branches, but the fire did not destroy the bush.

"God called out to him from the bush: Moses! Moses! He answered, 'Here I am.' God said: Do not come near! Remove your sandals from your feet, for the place where you stand is holy ground" (Exodus 3:4–5).

God spoke to Moses by showing him something amazing. But God does not only speak to people in the Bible. God speaks to all of us. By revealing himself in the burning bush, God shows that he does not always speak in words to us. God speaks to us deep in our hearts, through the grace of the Holy Spirit in us.

God also speaks to us through the gift of our conscience. Our conscience is always guiding us toward what is good and right. When we listen to our conscience, we can hear God speaking to us. God also speaks to us through his creation and through his Word in the Bible. Our prayer begins by listening to what God is saying to us. When we pray, we become aware that we are in God's presence. We listen to what he is saying.

## Activity

Write or draw about a time when you felt God's presence or heard God speaking in your heart.

**Prayer is an ongoing conversation with God.**

When God appeared to Moses in the burning bush, he told Moses that he had heard the cry of his people, the Israelites. They had been living in slavery in Egypt. God had a message for Moses:

"Now, go! I am sending you to Pharaoh to bring my people, the Israelites, out of Egypt. But Moses said to God, 'Who am I that I should go to Pharaoh and bring the Israelites out of Egypt?' God answered: I will be with you; and this will be your sign that I have sent you. When you have brought the people out of Egypt, you will serve God at this mountain. 'But,' said Moses to God, 'if I go to the Israelites and say to them, "The God of your ancestors has sent me to you," and they ask me, "What is his name?" what do I tell them?' God replied to Moses: I am who I am. Then he added: This is what you will tell the Israelites: I AM has sent me to you" (Exodus 3:10–14).

Do you notice something about how God and Moses spoke together? It was a conversation. Moses listened to what God said, and he responded honestly and with faith. He told God his concerns. When Moses was not sure what to do, he asked God for guidance and help. God showed Moses what he wanted him to do. God told Moses that he would always be with Moses to guide him.

In another part of this passage in Exodus, we read that "The LORD used to speak to Moses face to face, as a person speaks to a friend" (Exodus 33:11). Our prayer to God is a conversation, too. God knows everything about us. So we speak to God as a friend. Like Moses, we can be honest and truthful with God about our worries and concerns. We can ask him for what we need in faith.

When we ask God for good things, we are responding to what God wants for us.

## What Makes Us Catholic?

Sometimes it is hard to ask God for what we need. Yet even Jesus prayed to his Father when he needed help. As Catholics, when we pray to God for our needs, we show that we know we need *him*. We can pray to God in Jesus' name for help, for mercy, and for healing. We can also pray for good things to happen in our lives. There is no limit to our prayers. As pope, Saint John Paul II said: "Remember that you are never alone: Christ is with you on your journey every day of your lives! He has called you and chosen you to live in the freedom of the children of God. Turn to him in prayer and in love."

## We trust that God the Father hears our prayers.

The Israelites prayed a special prayer to God called the *Shema*. This is a Hebrew word that means "hear."

"Hear, O Israel!
The LORD is our God, the LORD alone!
Therefore, you shall love the LORD, your God, with your whole heart, and with your whole being, and with your whole strength" (Deuteronomy 6:4–5).

This prayer is based on the Ten Commandments. It is about trusting God. Jesus trusted his Father completely. He spent a great deal of time in prayer. Jesus wanted us to be like him. He wanted us to love others the way we love God. Jesus added to this prayer when he said: "'You shall love your neighbor as yourself.' There is no other commandment greater" (Mark 12:31).

Jesus wanted us to seek good things for ourselves and our neighbors. Because God blesses us, we can "bless" or praise and glorify him. He is the source of all our blessings. In our prayer, we can:

- praise God and give him our love and respect
- ask God to help us love others as he loves us
- ask God to forgive us when we have turned away from him
- thank God for being with us and for giving us all we need
- bless God our Father.

## Activity

Jesus would have prayed the *Shema*. Fill in the blanks to complete the prayer.

Hear, O _____!

The LORD is our God,
the LORD alone!

Therefore, you shall _____ the LORD, your God, with your whole _____, and with your whole being, and with your whole _____.

Memorize the prayer, as Jesus did. Pray it out loud with other members of your group.

## Partners in Faith

### Saint Rita

Saint Rita had a difficult life, yet she always trusted that God would hear her prayer. She trusted that God would keep her family from sin. We ask Rita to pray for us when things seem impossible.

 **Learn more about the life of Saint Rita.**

| **Faith Word** |
| prayer |

 **Show What You Know**

Read the statements. Circle whether the statement is True or False.
Correct any false statements you find.

**1.** Prayer is our response to God's call. True / False

_____

_____

**2.** When we ask God for good things, we are being selfish. True / False

_____

_____

**3.** Moses had an argument with God. True / False

_____

_____

## Live Your Faith

• In what ways can you listen better for God speaking to your heart?

_____

_____

_____

_____

_____

• In prayer, we can ask God for good things for others. What good things
for others will you ask God to do or give this week?

_____

_____

_____

_____

_____

_____

_____

## Mini-Task

There are many ways to pray. One type of prayer is called a prayer of petition. Petition means we ask God to help us with our wants and needs. Asking God for help in prayer does not mean that God will always answer us in the way we want him to. We trust God to listen and respond to our deepest needs and longings, so that we can be who he created us to be and follow the teachings of his Son, Jesus.

In the space below, write a prayer of petition asking God for what you need most right now.

**Prayer of Petition**

_____

_____

_____

_____

_____

_____

_____

_____

 **Want to do more? Go to your Portfolio to continue this activity.**

 **At Home**

As a family, take time to speak to God honestly in prayer. Have your family members tell God about anything that is making them happy or sad. Pray a favorite prayer, and listen to what God is saying to your family through the words.

# Why do we pray?

We pray because the Holy Spirit calls us to pray. We pray to grow into the people God created us to be. When we pray at all times and in all places, our love and trust in God grows. We find joy as followers of Christ.

**Go to the digital portal for a *Lectio* and *Visio Divina* prayer.**

*"The goal of the prayer is of secondary importance; what matters above all is the relationship with the Father."*

Pope Francis

## The Holy Spirit helps us to pray.

Many people guide us in our lives. Teachers guide us at school, and parents guide us at home. But who guides us in our prayers? Someone might teach us the words to prayers. We might also be guided by the lives of holy people. This is good guidance for us. But how do we know how to truly speak to God? The Holy Spirit guides us in our prayer because he loves us. Deep in our hearts, the Holy Spirit is always working, guiding us to seek the good things of heaven.

The Holy Spirit lives in the Church. The teachings of Jesus and the Apostles are passed down to us in Sacred Tradition. This is the living Tradition that is always present. Sacred Tradition can help us understand how God speaks to us in our lives. This helps us ask God for what we truly need to grow in God's friendship and love.

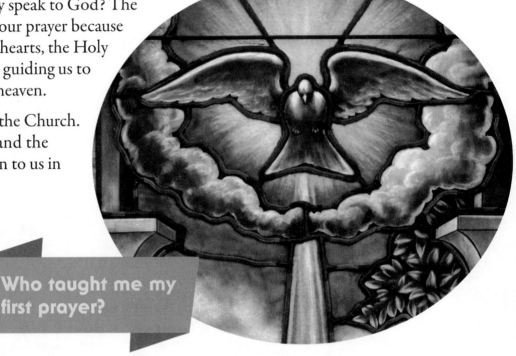

Who taught me my first prayer?

## What Makes Us Catholic?

The Society of St. Vincent de Paul in the United States is made up of almost one hundred thousand volunteers. Members of the society run thrift stores and food pantries that help to clothe and feed people in need. The society's House in a Box® program brings household items to people after a natural disaster. Whatever the need, members bring compassion and care to others. The Society of St. Vincent de Paul is active in more than four thousand communities in the United States.

## Did You Know?

**The whole Church prays together.**

## Prayer helps us do God's will.

To be **humble** means to be honest about ourselves and remember that it is God who gives us all good gifts. Jesus once told a parable about a way to be humble in our prayer:

"Two people went up to the temple area to pray; one was a Pharisee and the other was a tax collector. The Pharisee took up his position and spoke this prayer to himself, 'O God, I thank you that I am not like the rest of humanity—greedy, dishonest, adulterous—or even like this tax collector. I fast twice a week, and I pay tithes on my whole income.' But the tax collector stood off at a distance and would not even raise his eyes to heaven but beat his breast and prayed, 'O God, be merciful to me a sinner'" (Luke 18:10–13).

**Faith Word**

**humble** see p. 258

## Activity

Read the Parable of the Pharisee and the Tax Collector in Luke 18:9–14. Talk in small groups about how things would have happened in modern times. Think about these questions:

Who would be the person like the Pharisee?

What would the person like the Pharisee say he does each week?

What would he give away as a tithe?

Who would be the person like the tax collector?

What would the person like the tax collector pray at the end?

If we pray so that others will see us, or to show God how good we are, we are not really speaking to God as a friend. When we are ready to come to God with humble hearts, we can pray to seek God's will for our lives. God's will is what he wants for us. We can even ask God for a humble heart, so that we can grow in our prayer.

God wants us to live in his friendship, love, and peace. We do this by loving God and our neighbor. When we pray for strength to know and do God's will, our prayer is truly guided by God.

## One Church, Many Cultures

**A**ccording to Pope Francis, "peace-building is a process that calls us together." When we work for peace, we see every person as an important part of God's creation. Peacemakers help those who face hardships. For example, some Catholics in Australia help refugees who are hungry and homeless. Refugees are men, women, and children who had to leave their homes because of war. The group also promotes justice for people who are disabled. The group follows Jesus' example of helping those who are suffering.

## Prayer strengthens our relationship with the Blessed Trinity.

Prayer is not only about asking God to do things for us. We do not pray to try to change God's mind. We pray to change our minds and hearts. We pray for God's help in living the way God wants us to live.

In our prayer, we get to know God deeply. We think about the things God has said in his Word in the Bible. We come to know what God wants for us. We remember that God has created us in his divine image. What he wants for us is to be happy with him.

We are made to reflect God's holiness. God has given us many gifts to help us. He has given us a conscience to help us know what is right and wrong. As we work to form our conscience, we can pray that we will make good choices that reflect God's goodness and holiness in us.

### Activity

Prayer does not change God. Prayer changes us!

Write what you think this statement means.

_____

_____

_____

_____

_____

Gather in a small group and talk about your thoughts together. After you listened to other people's ideas, did you have any new thoughts? Write them down to remember them.

## Prayer strengthens us to live as Jesus' disciples.

God has placed the desire to seek him deep in our hearts. We find our true happiness in God, not in riches or fame or anything else. Jesus showed us a way to live that helps us find this happiness. The Beatitudes are at the center of Jesus' teaching. They help us seek God in everything we do and in everything that happens to us. When we seek God in prayer, we discover the way to live the blessed life Jesus promises in the Beatitudes and how to enter God's Kingdom.

Our prayer and our Christian living go hand in hand. We pray at all times. We follow Jesus at all times. We pray for strength and wisdom to live the Beatitudes. We pray for others so that they, too, can live the Beatitudes. This leads us and others closer to God.

## Partners in Faith
### Saint Vincent de Paul

Saint Vincent de Paul is known for his work with the poor. He is the inspiration for the Society of St. Vincent de Paul. He convinced wealthy people to help support his causes, which included establishing hospitals. He also worked tirelessly to encourage priests to become better pastors by giving retreats and by providing theological education.

 **Learn more about the life of Saint Vincent de Paul.**

## Faith Word

**humble**

 **Show What You Know**

Complete the sentences using the words in the word bank.

| will | Tradition | humble | hearts |

1. We do not pray to try to change God's mind. We pray to change our minds and _____.

2. Being _____ means being honest about ourselves and remembering that God gives us all good gifts.

3. God's _____ is what he wants for us.

4. Sacred _____ can help us understand how God speaks to us in our lives.

## Live Your Faith

• In what ways can you pray for strength and wisdom to live the Beatitudes?

_____

_____

_____

_____

_____

_____

_____

• What can having a humble heart bring to your prayer this week?

_____

_____

_____

_____

_____

_____

_____

## Mini-Task

True happiness is found in God. To live a happy life, we follow the teachings of Jesus and share his light and love with others. We give thanks to God in our prayers for every good thing he has given us.

What makes you happy? What gifts has God given you that help you live a happy, healthy, joy-filled life?

In the space below, design a happiness vision board. Draw, color, or cut out and paste pictures from a magazine.

**Happiness is in here.**

 **Want to do more? Go to your Portfolio to continue this activity.**

Talk with your family about what makes a humble heart. In what ways do your family members keep from comparing themselves with others? Pray together that you will always remember: God loves your family, just as you are.

# How do we pray?

There are many ways to pray. We can pray by ourselves or with others. We can pray out loud or in silence. We can bless, praise, and thank God. We can ask him for what we need and for what others need. We can find time every day to pray in some way to our loving God.

 **Go to the digital portal for a traditional prayer.**

*"But to you who hear I say, love your enemies, do good to those who hate you, bless those who curse you, pray for those who mistreat you."*

*Luke 6:27–28*

**Our prayers praise God and trust in his goodness.**

The Holy Spirit teaches us to pray. Here are the different kinds of prayers we can say:

- Prayers of *blessing* ask for God's favor and protection. For example, a parent may pray a blessing over his or her child at the start of the day.

- In prayers of *adoration*, we humble ourselves before the divinity of God. These are prayers of reverence and awe.

- In prayers of *petition* we ask God for something, either for ourselves or others.

- Prayers of *intercession* bring the needs of others to God. One of the ways we care for other people is to pray for their needs.

- Prayers of *thanksgiving* express gratitude for the favors God has bestowed on us.

- Prayers of *praise* acknowledge the glory of God. They express a deep love and respect for God and thank God for who and what he is.

God hears all of our prayers, no matter which kind of prayer we use.

What kind of prayer is in my heart right now?

## What Makes Us Catholic?

Every Catholic church has a tabernacle. This is a special place where the remaining Hosts from Holy Communion are kept. The Eucharist in the tabernacle is called the Blessed Sacrament. Catholics show their love for Jesus by kneeling in adoration before the Blessed Sacrament. They spend time praying to Jesus, truly present in the Blessed Sacrament. At certain times, the priest sets the Host in a special holder called a monstrance. He then carries the monstrance in a procession. Afterward, those gathered in the church can spend time in adoration of the Blessed Sacrament. Some churches participate in perpetual adoration. These churches allow people to pray before the Blessed Sacrament at any time—day or night. Look for the monstrance and tabernacle in your parish church.

# Did You Know?

**God hears and answers all prayers.**

## We can pray at all times.

Imagine seeing your best friend at school every day but only talking to your friend once a week. That would not make sense. God is with us always. So we talk to God every day in prayer. There are always things to talk to God about, and God has much he wants to say to us. Setting aside time each day helps us grow strong in the habit of regular prayer.

We can pray by ourselves. This is called personal prayer. We pray in the morning by offering up our day to God and asking the Holy Spirit to guide us in what we say, think, and do. We pray at night, sharing the events of our day with God. We look back at our day with God and ask him to show us how he was present or how we might have turned away from him. We ask him to help us do better tomorrow.

We also pray with others. We say prayers of blessing with our family before or after meals. Many families pray the Rosary together. The family is one of the first places where we learn when, how, and what to pray.

When we pray throughout our day, we allow God to order our day according to his will. We get strength to meet each day's challenges. We pray every day with trust in God, knowing he is always leading us to what is good.

## Activity

Think about the past week. Did you make time to pray?

Fill out the chart to plan times and ways to pray every day next week. Share your ideas with a friend.

| | Morning | Before Meals | Evening | Bedtime | Attend Mass |
|---|---|---|---|---|---|
| Sunday | | | | | |
| Monday | | | | | |
| Tuesday | | | | | |
| Wednesday | | | | | |
| Thursday | | | | | |
| Friday | | | | | |
| Saturday | | | | | |

## The Mass is the Church's greatest prayer.

God has not created us to be alone. He means for us to work, play, and pray together. We pray with one another and for one another. When we pray the prayers of the liturgy, we join with the entire Church.

Our celebration of the Eucharist is the heart of our Christian life and our prayer life. Catholics around the world gather to celebrate the Mass at all times of the day, every day. In the Eucharist, we are united with Christ and with one another. Together, as the Body of Christ, we bless, praise, and thank God. We can ask him for what we need and for what others need. The Eucharist is the most important prayer of the Church.

Another prayer that unites the Church is the Liturgy of the Hours. This prayer is part of the public prayer and work of the whole Church. It is made up of psalms, Scripture readings, prayers of intercession, hymns, and other prayers. The Liturgy of the Hours is prayed at certain times of the day and into the night. Whenever we take part in the Liturgy of the Hours, we pray on behalf of the whole Church.

## Activity

The Liturgy of the Hours is part of the public prayer of the Church. It is a way to pray at specific times during the day. Some of these times are:

1. Morning Prayer _____

_____

_____

2. Daytime Prayer _____

_____

_____

3. Evening Prayer _____

_____

_____

4. Night Prayer _____

_____

_____

On the lines above, write a short prayer that you could pray at each of these times.

## We can pray aloud or silently in our hearts.

Prayer is one of the ways we seek God, who has created us and loves us. Whether we pray out loud or in silence, our prayer comes from our hearts. There are two kinds of silent prayer: meditation and contemplation.

In **meditation**, we seek to understand how God is working in our lives and what he wants for us. We might meditate, or think, about Sacred Scripture. We can use our imagination to picture a scene in Scripture. We can also meditate on a holy image, such as the crucifix or one of the Stations of the Cross. We think about what is happening and we listen to what God is saying to us. We think about what this means in our own lives.

**Faith Word**

meditation see p. 258

Praying the Rosary is a way to meditate on events in the life of Jesus and Mary. As we say the prayers and picture the events— or mysteries of the Rosary—in our minds, we hold the rosary beads in our hands. We ask God to help us understand what these mysteries mean for us right now. Praying the Rosary helps us keep our minds, hearts, and bodies focused on our prayer.

### One Church, Many Cultures

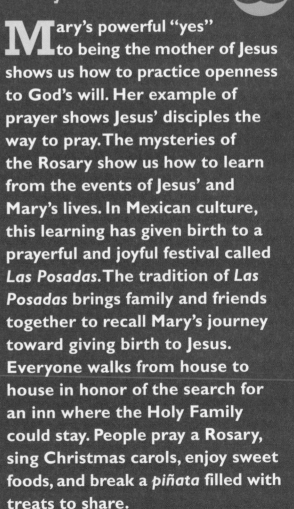

**M**ary's powerful "yes" to being the mother of Jesus shows us how to practice openness to God's will. Her example of prayer shows Jesus' disciples the way to pray. The mysteries of the Rosary show us how to learn from the events of Jesus' and Mary's lives. In Mexican culture, this learning has given birth to a prayerful and joyful festival called *Las Posadas*. The tradition of *Las Posadas* brings family and friends together to recall Mary's journey toward giving birth to Jesus. Everyone walks from house to house in honor of the search for an inn where the Holy Family could stay. People pray a Rosary, sing Christmas carols, enjoy sweet foods, and break a *piñata* filled with treats to share.

## Faith Word

contemplation see p. 257

Contemplation is another form of silent prayer. In contemplation, we become aware of Christ's loving presence. Some people describe contemplative prayer as simply gazing at God in faith and love. We do not have to use memorized prayers, but we can if it helps us. In contemplation, we allow Jesus to come into our hearts. We can be with Jesus in this way, just as we might sit with a friend or loved one without needing to say anything.

One form of contemplation is Eucharistic adoration. This is spending time in the presence of Jesus Christ in the Blessed Sacrament. In many churches, the Blessed Sacrament is displayed in a special vessel called a monstrance. People come to pray and spend time with Jesus throughout the day and even at night.

## Partners in Faith

### Saint Elizabeth of Portugal

Saint Elizabeth was Queen of Portugal. She prayed the Divine Office every day to give her strength to complete her duties. She attended daily Mass and said it helped her in difficult times. Saint Elizabeth was often asked to make peace in her family. Other countries asked her to help with peace treaties.

 **Learn more about the life of Saint Elizabeth of Portugal.**

| Faith Words | |
|---|---|
| meditation | contemplation |

 **Show What You Know**

In your own words, write definitions for the terms.

**meditation**

_____

_____

_____

_____

**prayers of intercession**

_____

_____

_____

_____

**contemplation**

_____

_____

_____

_____

## Live Your Faith

• Which of the forms of prayer—blessing, adoration, petition, intercession, thanksgiving, and praise—do you pray most often? Why?

_____

_____

_____

• Is it easier for you to pray silently or out loud? Why?

_____

_____

_____

## How do I pray for others?

# Mini-Task

One of the ways we care for others is to bring their needs before God. Prayers of intercession are a reminder that other people need God's love and healing, too. We often say "I'm praying for you" when something bad happens. Do we make good on our promise to pray for other people?

In the space below, draft a note to friends or family members in which you say you are praying for them, and tell them why. Take a moment to pray for them now!

_____

_____

_____

_____

_____

_____

_____

_____

_____

_____

_____

 **Want to do more? Go to your Portfolio to continue this activity.**

# At Home

Ask your family members about the ways they pray during the week. What kind of prayer helps each of them feel closest to God?

# What helps us to pray?

We have many gifts to help us pray. We have our own families, and we have the family of the Church: the Communion of Saints. They pray with us and for us. We also have God's Word, the Church's liturgy, and the virtues of faith, hope, and charity. With so many good people and good things to help us, we can pray at all times and in all places.

 **Go to the digital portal for a prayer of praise.**

*"And we have this confidence in him, that if we ask anything according to his will, he hears us."*

*1 John 5:14*

## The Church is strengthened and guided by holy men and women.

Throughout the centuries, holy people have found ways to seek and follow Jesus.

Saint Anthony wanted to follow the command Jesus gave to the rich young man in the Gospel of Matthew: "If you wish to be perfect, go, sell what you have and give to [the] poor, and you will have treasure in heaven. Then come, follow me" (Matthew 19:21). Anthony gave everything he owned to the poor. He went to the desert to live a life of prayer and fasting. Eventually others joined Anthony. They became known as the Desert Fathers. They lived simple lives of quiet prayer. Their wisdom has been passed on through many generations.

Saint Benedict of Nursia created a way of living that included regular times for prayer and work. It gave the monks of his monasteries rhythm and balance for their days. It is known as the *Rule of Saint Benedict*. It is still used by many people today.

Saint Francis of Assisi was inspired by God to live a life of prayer and joyful poverty so that he could depend on God completely. Followers of Saint Francis are called Franciscans.

**Faith Word**

**Christian spirituality**
see p. 257

Saint Ignatius of Loyola gave us a way to pray known as the *Spiritual Exercises*. He founded a religious order known as the Society of Jesus, or the Jesuits.

**Christian spirituality** involves finding God through prayer, Scripture, and Sacred Tradition. It always puts Jesus Christ at the center of everything. We can learn from Christian spirituality ways that we can follow Jesus in our own lives. We can learn methods of prayer that can help us grow in our love for God and our neighbors.

In what ways can I make more time for prayer every day?

## Did You Know?

 **The desire to know God is part of human nature.**

## The virtues of faith, hope, and charity are sources of prayer.

The virtues of faith, hope, and charity (or love) are gifts that God has given us to help us live and pray. Faith leads us to seek God and his plan for us. We can pray with faith in God because we have signs of God's presence among us. God is present to us in Sacred Scripture and Tradition, and in the life of the Church. We know that the Blessed Trinity—Father, Son, and Holy Spirit—loves us and remains with us always. God's greatest sign of his presence is his Son, Jesus. Through faith, we can know and believe in these signs of God's presence and love.

The Holy Spirit guides us to pray in hope. We pray with hope in God's love and mercy. Hope is what helps us look forward to our eternal life with God. We remember that the Beatitudes promise we are blessed when we live the life God wants for us. Even if we are sad or poor or persecuted, hope reminds us that we are blessed. We are promised God's life of eternal happiness and peace.

## What Makes Us Catholic?

Hopeful, joyful prayer is an important part of Catholic prayer life. When we pray the Rosary, for example, we can meditate on the joyful events in the lives of Jesus and Mary. The five Joyful Mysteries are: the Annunciation, the Visitation, the Nativity, the Presentation of Jesus in the Temple, and the Finding of Jesus in the Temple. As we celebrate each mystery, we think about what it means to us. And we pray that others experience the joy of Jesus' presence in their lives.

## Activity

Schools of spirituality show us ways to live and pray. Read the terms below, which are qualities of different schools of spirituality. Circle the ones that interest you.

| | |
|---|---|
| simplicity | service to the poor |
| meditation | active work |
| reading the Bible | singing or playing an instrument |
| Eucharistic adoration | community |

In what ways can the things you circled be a part of your work for God?

God is love. His love is poured into our hearts by the Holy Spirit. This is why we say that love is the source of prayer. We pray with the knowledge that God has loved us always. His love for us never ends. When we know that we are loved by God, we can respond to him by reflecting his love to others. We love all people because they are made in God's image. We pray with hearts full of love for God and for others.

When we pray with the virtues of faith, hope, and charity, we grow in our understanding of God, ourselves, and others. When we pray every day, through even the simplest, most ordinary things that happen to us, we begin to see the events of our lives as God sees them. Through our prayer, we start to see how God wants us to live. We are able to work with Jesus to know, love, and serve the Father more every day. In this way, we work with Jesus to bring about the Kingdom of God.

## Activity

Join two other friends. One of you represents the virtue of faith. The second person represents the virtue of hope. The third represents the virtue of charity, or love. Prepare a role play in which you explain to the group what your virtue is, what it does, and how it helps us know and love God. Explain how all three virtues work together with the help of the Holy Spirit when we pray.

## Prayer strengthens Christian family life.

Prayer is part of our Christian family life. Many people learn their first prayers at home, from their parents. Our prayers help us understand that God is our Father and we are part of his family. The prayers that we learn as children all inspire us to love and care for our families. From there, we learn how to love and care for others.

It is good to memorize prayers and keep them in your heart. You can think about the prayers you memorize and allow the Holy Spirit to help you understand what they mean. Even if you don't understand some prayers completely right now, you can have faith that you will understand more later. You will be glad you have memorized prayers. The prayers we memorize can be like stepping stones toward deeper understanding of God, ourselves, and others.

As we grow in our prayer, we grow in the virtues of faith, hope, and charity. We see ourselves and others more clearly as God's children, made in God's image. We learn new ways of loving and serving God and others. We are drawn closer to God and the blessed life of happiness he wants for us.

### One Church, Many Cultures

The word *charity* might make you think of just giving money or goods to help people. Yet charity means "love." The Church's good works begin and end with love for the people she helps. Missionaries like the Missionaries of Charity travel to many continents to care for people and show them that they are not forgotten. No matter where we are in the world, the virtue of charity helps Catholics to love and serve people. The love of Christ is within us. When we serve others, we show his love for those people, too.

## Prayer turns our hearts toward God.

At times, it can be hard for us to pray. Sometimes this is because we do not fully understand what prayer is, or we forget what it is. Prayer is a gift of God's grace. It is our response to the Holy Spirit working in us. When we pray, we let the Holy Spirit guide us.

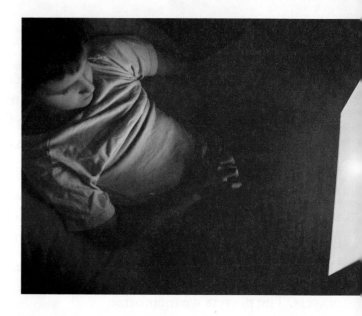

Sometimes we find it difficult to pray because we are thinking about other things (such as playing with friends or going to the movies). These distractions can be activities we think we would rather be doing. They can be problems or worries. All of these distractions show us what we might be putting before God. To move past them, we can pray humbly to God. We can ask him to help us turn away from our distractions or the concerns that bother us. We can ask God to help us put him first in our lives. Every day, we ask God to turn our hearts toward him.

We have learned that God is always calling us to conversion, to turn toward him. It is not difficult to respond to God's call to prayer.

We can simply speak to him in honesty, as a friend who loves us. We can tell God what is on our minds. God knows that we are not perfect. When we bring our problems and sins to God, God gives us the grace to turn away from them. He shows us how to live. The more we pray, the closer God draws us to himself. The more we live our lives the way God has planned for us, the more we can truly be happy.

## Partners in Faith
### Saint Frances of Rome

Saint Frances of Rome had a long and happy marriage. Frances spent much of her time taking care of her husband, who had been injured in a war. She used herbs and natural medicines, but she gave God the credit for her success in healing illnesses. Saint Frances fully lived family life and spiritual life.

 **Learn more about the life of Saint Frances of Rome.**

## Faith Word

**Christian spirituality**

 ## Show What You Know

Circle the correct term to complete the sentence.

1. Prayer is a gift of God's _____.

   **a.** children

   **b.** grace

   **c.** wisdom

2. Christian _____ involves finding God through prayer, Scripture, and Sacred Tradition.

   **a.** school

   **b.** initiation

   **c.** spirituality

3. Prayer turns our hearts toward _____.

   **a.** our friends

   **b.** God

   **c.** our problems

Fill in the blanks to complete the paragraph.

The virtues help us to pray. We can pray with _____ in God because we have signs of God's presence among us. We pray with _____ in God's love and mercy. We can pray with hearts full of _____ for God and for others.

## Live Your Faith

• What sometimes distracts you from prayer? In what ways do you ask God to help you pray?

_____

_____

_____

• What virtue is most helpful to you when you are praying? Why?

_____

_____

_____

What helps me to pray?

## Mini-Task

Sometimes it is difficult to pray. In these times, it can be helpful to repeat one word in prayer over and over again. For example, you could repeat the word *Jesus* quietly for one minute. (Or try these words: *light, love, help, listen,* or *trust.*) Our Catholic prayer tradition uses repetition as a way to focus on God and remember what matters most in our lives.

Write down a few words you may want to use as prayer words. Then design a word cloud prayer using your words.

_____                    _____

_____                    _____

_____        JESUS

                                           _____

_____

                _____

 **Want to do more? Go to your Portfolio to continue this activity.**

During prayer, we talk and listen to God and are formed as his disciples. As a family, practice listening in a quiet place. Turn off any devices that might distract you. Begin by being quiet for at least two minutes, and then work up to a longer period. Remind your family that the quieter we are, the better we can listen to God.

# Why is the Lord's Prayer called the perfect prayer?

If you want to know what Jesus teaches, look at the Lord's Prayer. This is the perfect prayer because it contains everything Jesus has taught us. In the Lord's Prayer, we love and honor God as our Father. We pray for the coming of God's Kingdom. We pray to live as Jesus lived, in love and mercy.

**Go to the digital portal for a traditional prayer.**

*"Your Father knows what you need before you ask him."*

Matthew 6:8

## Jesus himself taught us the Lord's Prayer.

Jesus showed us the perfect way to live when he taught us the Beatitudes. In the **Lord's Prayer**, he showed us the perfect way to pray. The prayer Jesus taught, which we also call the Our Father, sums up everything Jesus taught in the Gospels.

We begin Jesus' prayer with the words *Our Father*. This reminds us of the Good News that Jesus brings us: that we are brothers and sisters in Christ, the Son of God. Through

### Faith Word

**Lord's Prayer** see p. 258

Jesus, we can speak to God as our Father. We can speak and act toward one another as members of God's family, all created in God's image.

We say the Lord's Prayer together at the celebration of the Mass and the sacraments to remind us of how to live as followers of Christ.

How do I address God when I pray?

## Did You Know?

 **The Lord's Prayer is probably the most influential prayer on earth.**

## The Lord's Prayer helps us know God.

When God appeared to Moses in the burning bush, Moses asked who he was. God said "I AM." This answer tells us that God has always existed and will exist forever. God is the Creator of all things. God is perfect goodness, holiness, and love. All of this is difficult for us to understand. But Jesus reveals God as his Father. In the Lord's Prayer, he calls God "*our* Father." God is our loving, perfect Father, whose goodness is without end. We are happy to have such a Father.

God has created each of us in his own image. We are created to be good, holy, and loving, just as God is. In the Lord's Prayer, we ask God to help us live as a reflection of his goodness and love. We ask God to help us live as Jesus' disciples.

## What Makes Us Catholic?

The Lord's Prayer is the most perfect prayer. It is part of many of our more elaborate Catholic prayers and devotions, such as the Rosary and the Chaplet of Divine Mercy. We also pray the Our Father when celebrating the sacraments. In Baptism, for example, the community prays the Lord's Prayer together before the final blessing. It is also an important part of the celebration of the Eucharist, during the Mass. At Mass this Sunday, pay attention to when everyone stands to pray the Lord's Prayer. You might want to add the Lord's Prayer before or after a prayer you already pray during the week.

## Activity

Choose one line or phrase from the Our Father. Write or illustrate what you think that line or phrase means.

## In the Lord's Prayer we honor and praise God.

In the Lord's Prayer, Jesus tells us that God is our Father. He also reveals who we are: we are God's children. In our Baptism, we become adopted children of God and, therefore, brothers and sisters of Jesus Christ, the Son of God. We become co-heirs to the Kingdom of God. We join all of God's people, living as one Body in Christ—the Church.

As God's sons and daughters, we want to honor God. We pray that all people will honor the name of God when we say "**hallowed** be thy name." The best way we can honor God is by living according to his will. This means living the way Jesus taught us. We must place God above all things.

**Faith Word**

**hallowed** see p. 257

## Activity

Work in pairs or small groups to fill in the chart. List two or three names for God that you have learned. Then write two more names you could give God.

| When we say: | Names for God I know | Other names I can call God |
|---|---|---|
| **Our Father, who art in heaven, hallowed be thy name.** | | |

Compare your chart with the chart of another pair or group.

We pray for the coming of God's Kingdom when we say "thy Kingdom come." We are asking to help bring about God's Kingdom of love, peace, and joy. We are asking God to help us be poor in spirit.

God wants all of us to live in joy and peace with him forever. This is God's will for us. When we pray that "God's will be done on earth as it is in heaven," we are asking that God's providence extend throughout the created order. We are asking God to help us know how to live according to his will and the example of Jesus. Jesus teaches us that we enter the Kingdom of Heaven and eternal happiness with God not by speaking words, but by doing "the will of my Father in heaven" (Matthew 7:21).

## One Church, Many Cultures

All people mattered to Jesus. He did not measure their value by what they looked like or how they spoke. All people are God's children. This principle is explained in the Catholic social teaching called *Solidarity of the Human Family*. Solidarity means knowing that we are all members of the one human family. We show solidarity when we work to help people near or far away who may be suffering. We show solidarity when we love all people, no matter what their racial or cultural backgrounds are. This principle helps us promote God's Kingdom of love, peace, and joy in everything we say and do.

## The Lord's Prayer helps us place our trust in God.

How can we bring about God's Kingdom? In the Lord's Prayer we ask for strength to do this. We ask God to make us able to honor him as he deserves to be honored. We also ask God to "give us this day our daily bread." We trust that God will give us food and the other material things that we need to live and grow. But we are also asking for the Bread from Heaven that is Jesus Christ in the Eucharist. When we receive Jesus in the Eucharist, we gain strength for living the Beatitudes every day.

We ask God to "forgive us our trespasses, as we forgive those who trespass against us." God's forgiveness frees us to live as his disciples. In the Sacrament of Penance and Reconciliation, we receive God's sacramental grace to strengthen or restore the sanctifying grace we received at Baptism.

We ask God to open our hearts to his grace so that we can forgive others. As we show mercy to others, God shows mercy to us. We also ask God to "lead us not into temptation, but deliver us from evil." Our prayer is that God will keep us strong when we face the temptation to sin. We pray that we will use God's gift of conscience to help us make the right choices.

We pray the Our Father in the trust that God will guide us and give us the strength we need so that we can live in his kingdom of righteousness, joy, and peace forever.

## Partners in Faith

### Blessed Jerzy Popiełuszko

Blessed Jerzy Popiełuszko was a Polish priest. He was opposed to Communism and spoke out against it. Despite being arrested, he continued to protest. His strong faith and prayer life gave him the courage to stand up. He is a national hero in Poland.

 **Learn more about the life of Blessed Jerzy Popiełuszko.**

**Faith Words**

**Faith Words**

**Lord's Prayer**     **hallowed**

 ## Show What You Know

Match the terms to the correct descriptions.

**1.** Lord's Prayer

**2.** hallowed

**3.** Bread from Heaven

the Eucharist

the prayer that sums up everything
Jesus taught in the Gospels; also called
the Our Father

holy or sacred

## Live Your Faith

- In what way would you explain why the Lord's Prayer is a perfect prayer to
someone who has never heard it?

_____

_____

_____

_____

_____

_____

- In what way does knowing you are a child of God make it easier to pray
the Lord's Prayer?

_____

_____

_____

_____

_____

_____

_____

## Mini-Task

Christians all over the world pray the Lord's Prayer. Do you know the Lord's Prayer in another language? If so, share that with the group.

Look up the Lord's Prayer in other languages, such as Spanish, German, and French. How do you say "Our Father" in Spanish? In German? In French? In sign language? Write the words *Our Father* in a few different languages below. Then try to say them out loud or pray them in sign language.

### "Our Father" around the World

1. _____

2. _____

3. _____

4. _____

5. _____

6. _____

7. _____

8. _____

 **Want to do more? Go to your Portfolio to continue this activity.**

# At Home

As a family, make a prayer card or poster with the words of the Our Father. Decorate it with symbols or other images that are special to your family. Underline the parts of the prayer that mean the most to you. The next time you pray together, have the card with you.

**Liturgical Calendar**

Easter

Triduum

Lent

Ordinary Time

Christmas

Advent

Ordinary Time

EQUATOR

MAY · JUN · JUL · AUG · SEP · OCT · NOV · DEC · JAN · FEB · MAR · APR

In the liturgical year, the date of Easter Sunday, the celebration of our Lord's Resurrection, depends each year on the spring equinox and the rising of the full moon. Easter Sunday follows the full moon after the spring equinox. The spring equinox is the day on which the sun crosses the equator, making day and night of equal length everywhere. Thus, the timing of Easter Sunday reminds us that our Lord's Resurrection brings light to our darkness.

Astronomers can calculate the date of the spring equinox. Looking at their calculations, we find that Easter Sunday is always between March 22 and April 25. Using the date for Easter Sunday, each year's unique liturgical calendar can be determined.

# Unit Prayer

**Leader:** One of Saint Teresa of Ávila's best-known teachings reminds us that we are the Body of Christ on earth. We are his hands, feet, and eyes. We are the living Christ here on earth.

Let us listen to missionary disciples who are living as the hands, feet, and eyes of Christ today.

Let us pray:

Dear Jesus, we ask you to help us be your Body now in this world. Through the Mass and the seasons of the Church year, we are able to know how much you love us and want us to be your disciples.

We thank you for teaching us how to live in your holy Word.

**All:** We are your hands now on earth.

**Leader:** Help us bring your care to others.

**All:** We are your feet now on earth.

**Leader:** Guide us to those in most need of our love and service.

**All:** We are your eyes now on earth.

**Leader:** Help us to see suffering and injustice and respond with mercy.

**All:** We are your Body now on earth.

**Leader:** Let us pray the Lord's Prayer. Our Father, . . .

*End the Unit Prayer by singing the song for this unit.*

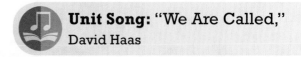

**Unit Song:** "We Are Called," David Haas

## Missionary Discipleship

When have you been the hands of Christ? His feet? His eyes? How did you feel?

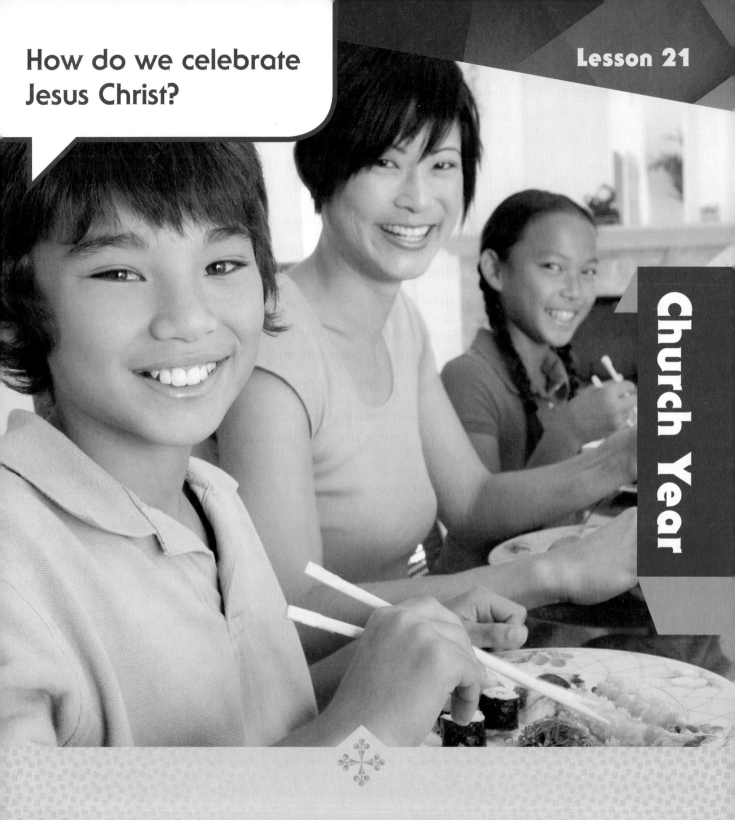

## How do we celebrate Jesus Christ?

**Church Year**

*"My mother and my brothers are those who hear the word of God and act on it."*

Luke 8:21

# Gathering Prayer

**Leader:** We offer thanks to God during the liturgical year in many different ways. We follow in the footsteps of Jesus through the many seasons that we celebrate. Our lives are changed at Mass through the Word, the Eucharist, and each other.

O Lord, we celebrate your love for us every Sunday at Mass.

**All:** O Lord, we celebrate your love for us every Sunday at Mass.

**Leader:** In Advent, let your light shine in our hearts as we hear about your coming in your Word.

**All:** O Lord, we celebrate your love for us every Sunday at Mass.

**Leader:** At Christmas, let your birth fill our hearts with joy and peace, and help us share it with one another at Mass.

**All:** O Lord, we celebrate your love for us every Sunday at Mass.

**Leader:** During Lent, Triduum, and Easter, help us share in the beauty and power of these liturgies that tell of your great love for us all.

**All:** O Lord, we celebrate your love for us every Sunday at Mass.

## Activity

Take a look at the liturgical year calendar. Count how many Sundays are in each season of the Church year.

**Advent:**          **Easter:**          **Lent:**

**Christmas:**       **Ordinary Time:**

As a group, talk about why some seasons might be longer than others.

**The liturgical year celebrates God's saving work through his Son, Jesus.**

The seasons of the Church year are Advent, Christmas, Lent, Triduum, Easter, and Ordinary Time. The seasons celebrate the life and work of Jesus Christ, his birth, his Death and Resurrection, and the sending of the Holy Spirit. In addition to these seasons, there are also special feast days in the Church year that honor Mary and the saints.

The calendar of the saints varies from country to country, because each land and people has saints who are special to them. Some examples of American saints are Elizabeth Ann Seton and Kateri Tekakwitha. There are also saints who are celebrated universally, in every place. Some examples would be saints named in the New Testament, such as Peter and Paul, and Mary Magdalene. Some very popular saints, such as Francis of Assisi, are also celebrated everywhere.

Mary, the Mother of Jesus, is honored on many days, several of which are Holy Days of Obligation in the United States. The most solemn celebrations of Mary are on January 1 (Mary, Mother of God), August 15 (the Assumption of Mary into heaven), and December 8 (the Immaculate Conception of Mary). She is the most highly honored of all the saints and first among Jesus' disciples.

## Did You Know?

 **The saints were ordinary people who lived extraordinary lives.**

Each saint has a different story, yet all of them are part of the distinguished history of the Church. They are remembered because they were faithful to Jesus and helped to spread the Kingdom of God. Their example and prayers help us to be faithful, too.

Celebrations of the saints can brighten the Church year. Colorful local customs that honor the saints, such as processions, pilgrimages, or parades, express our joy and our faith in God.

**Church Year**

---

## Activity

Find your birthday on the liturgical year calendar. Look up what saint is celebrated on that day. Write your name and the saint's name on the date in the calendar.

As a class, recite a litany of saints who share your birthdays.

*Saint* _____, *pray for us.*

# Readers Theater

## The Wedding at Cana

(Based on John 2:1–11)

### Roles: Narrator 1, Narrator 2, Jesus, Mary, Headwaiter

*"Do whatever he tells you."*

**Narrator 1:** Weddings are ceremonies of great joy and celebration. Everyone wants to have a wonderful time toasting the bride and groom. This is true now, and it was true when Jesus and his disciples were invited to a wedding in Cana in Galilee. Mary, the Mother of Jesus, was also there.

**Narrator 2:** All were enjoying the food and drink when it was noted that the wine was running out. Mary turned to Jesus.

**Mary:** "They have no wine" (John 2:3).

**Jesus:** "Woman, how does your concern affect me? My hour has not yet come" (John 2:4).

**Narrator 1:** During this time, calling his mother "Woman" was not a sign of disrespect. It would be like saying "Ma'am." We might say that Jesus is respectfully asking his mother: "Why should this concern us?"

**Narrator 2:** The wedding occurred early in Jesus' ministry. He had not yet performed his many miracles. The first would occur now. Mary spoke directly to the servers.

**Mary:** "Do whatever he tells you" (John 2:5).

**Narrator 1:** Within the house holding the wedding reception, there were six large stone water jars. Each jar could hold between twenty and thirty gallons. Jesus addressed the servers.

**Jesus:** "Fill the jars with water" (John 2:7).

**Narrator 2:** The servers did what they were told and filled each jar up to the top. Jesus instructed the servers:

**Jesus:** "Draw some out now and take it to the headwaiter" (John 2:8).

**Narrator 1:** The servers again did what Jesus told them to do. They took the sample to the headwaiter, who tasted the water and found it had become wine. The headwaiter did not know where such wine had come from, but the servers knew.

**Narrator 2:** At once, the headwaiter called over to the bridegroom.

**Headwaiter:** "Everyone serves good wine first, . . . but you have kept the good wine until now" (John 2:10).

**Narrator 1:** The miracle of turning water into wine at the wedding in Cana was the first sign that revealed Jesus' glory. "[A]nd his disciples began to believe in him" (John 2:11).

How is Jesus a part of my life all year?

## Mini-Task

The seasons of the Church year help us celebrate Jesus' life and work. All year long, we are called to do Jesus' work in the world.

Each time you learn about a season of the Church year, you will think of a way to serve others that young people could do in that season.

Think about the Church year. Brainstorm ideas for a service that young people could perform, inspired by Jesus' teachings or the work of the saints. Record your best idea in the chart below.

| Church Year Service Ministry | |
|---|---|
| **Whom or what will this serve?** | |
| **What service will you provide?** | |
| **Where and when will the service take place?** | |
| **Why is this service important?** | |

Discuss your idea with a partner. Share suggestions for ways your idea could be put into action.

 **Want to do more? Go to your Portfolio to continue this activity.**

 **At Home**

Is there a saint who has a particular meaning to your family? Talk together about what that saint means to you or about times when you could pray to the saints for their help.

## Why does Jesus come to save us?

**Advent**

"*Behold, I am sending my messenger ahead of you; he will prepare your way.*"

*Mark 1:2*

# Gathering Prayer

**Leader:** In the season of Advent, we prepare to celebrate Jesus' coming again into our world and wait in joyful hope for his birth at Christmas. The prophet Isaiah spoke of Emmanuel, which means "God with us."

We will pray: "Rejoice, rejoice, Emmanuel, shall come to you, O Israel."

**All:** "Rejoice, rejoice, Emmanuel, shall come to you, O Israel."

**Leader:** Lord Jesus, prepare a place in our hearts for your return. Come to us, Emmanuel.

**All:** "Rejoice, rejoice, Emmanuel, shall come to you, O Israel."

**Leader:** Lord Jesus, fill us with your love as we wait for your return. Come to us, Emmanuel.

**All:** "Rejoice, rejoice, Emmanuel, shall come to you, O Israel."

**Leader:** O God, we rejoice that you became one of us, that you sent us your Son, Jesus. Come to us, Emmanuel.

**All:** "Rejoice, rejoice, Emmanuel, shall come to you, O Israel."

## Activity

We prepare our hearts during Advent. Write on the heart one way you can prepare your heart for Christ's return.

As a group, choose one way to prepare for each week of Advent. Place a list of ideas next to a classroom Advent wreath.

## Our hearts look forward to the coming of Christ.

Advent is a season of joy and hopeful waiting for the coming of the Savior. It is a time to pray, reflect, and prepare our hearts to celebrate Jesus' birth more than two thousand years ago. We also wait for him to come again at the end of time.

Each season of the liturgical year has its own distinct color. We see this color in the priest's vestments at Mass and also in church decorations. The color of Advent is violet (purple). On the third Sunday of Advent, the priest may wear a rose-colored vestment. We also light the pink candle of the Advent wreath on this Sunday as a sign of joy.

In Advent, we learn about John the Baptist, who called people to change their lives. His message is one that we hear in the Gospel readings during Advent. He said: "Prepare the way of the Lord" (Mark 1:3).

When we prepare our hearts for Christ's return, we share in the joy and the hope that his birth brought to the world. God's people had waited a long time for a Savior to come.

Jesus' birth would change everything for them. His birth changes us, too.

During the season of Advent, through prayer and reflection on the Gospels, we prepare for the joyful coming of Jesus. We prepare the way of the Lord in our hearts and minds.

## Did You Know?

 **Jesus' birth changed everything.**

**Advent**

## Activity

Prepare a word web of all the things you know about Advent.

```
  (_____)            (_____)
         \             /
          \           /
           (  Advent  )
          /           \
         /             \
  (_____)            (_____)
```

Add your ideas to a class word web on a whiteboard.

# Advent Prayer Ritual

 **"Christ, Circle Round Us,"**
Dan Schutte

*Prayer before the Advent wreath:*

**Leader:** In the name of the Father, and of the Son, and of the Holy Spirit. Amen.

Let us listen to a reading from Sacred Scripture from the Gospel of Mark.

"A voice of one crying out in the desert: 'Prepare the way of the Lord, make straight his paths'" (Mark 1:3).

**All:** Prepare the way of the Lord; make straight his paths.

**Leader:** As we stand around the Advent wreath, let us ask Jesus to help us shine his light in us more brightly in our world.

We pray for the Church and her leaders, who guide us on the pathway to the love of God.

**All:** Prepare the way of the Lord; make straight his paths.

**Leader:** We pray for all government officials, that they look after our country to promote peace and justice for all of its people.

**All:** Prepare the way of the Lord; make straight his paths.

**Leader:** We pray for those who are suffering, that the light of Advent lifts them from the darkness of their lives.

**All:** Prepare the way of the Lord; make straight his paths.

**Leader:** And let us pray for all who are in our parish, that Jesus will be born again in their hearts this Christmas.

**All:** Prepare the way of the Lord; make straight his paths.

**Leader:** I invite each of you to offer a prayer in the silence of your heart, that this Advent will be a time of peace and joy as you prepare for the coming of Jesus.

(*The students offer their prayers.*)

**All:** Prepare the way of the Lord; make straight his paths.

What can I do to celebrate the birth of Jesus?

## Mini-Task

During the season of Advent, we look forward with hope to the birth of Jesus.

Think about what we celebrate during Advent. Brainstorm ideas for service that young people could do as we wait for the birth of Jesus. Record your best idea in the chart below.

| Advent Service Ministry | |
| --- | --- |
| **Whom or what will this serve?** | |
| **What service will you provide?** | |
| **Where will you do the service?** | |
| **When will the service take place?** | |
| **Why is this service important?** | |
| **How does this service connect to Advent?** | |

Discuss your idea with a partner. Share suggestions for ways your idea could be put into action.

 **Want to do more? Go to your Portfolio to continue this activity.**

# At Home

As a family, talk about events that have changed you, like the birth or death of family members, or a move to a new community. Talk about ways that Jesus' birth has changed each of you and the world.

How did the Son of God enter human history?

Christmas

*"For a child is born to us, a son is given to us; . . . They name him Wonder-Counselor, God-Hero, Father-Forever, Prince of Peace."*

Isaiah 9:5

# Gathering Prayer

**Leader:** In the season of Christmas, we celebrate the birth of Jesus. He is the very presence of God in human form. God loves us so much that he became one of us to teach us how to live and share in God's love.

**All:** All the ends of the earth have seen the power of God.

**Leader:** A light has shone on us this Christmas, as promised by the prophets in Scripture. Let us be glad and rejoice!

**All:** All the ends of the earth have seen the power of God.

**Leader:** Christ our King was born in a stable, surrounded by animals and straw. God lives among the rich and poor. Let us be glad and rejoice!

**All:** All the ends of the earth have seen the power of God.

**Leader:** We ask Mary to help us say "yes" to God's call in our daily lives. Let us be glad and rejoice!

**All:** All the ends of the earth have seen the power of God.

**Leader:** With the choir of angels that sang at the birth of Jesus, we sing:

**All:** "Glory to God in the highest and on earth peace to those on whom his favor rests" (Luke 2:14).

## Activity

Work in small groups to read the account of the Nativity in Luke 2:1–20. Fill in the chart with what you learn.

| | |
|---|---|
| **Who was present?** | |
| **What were they doing?** | |
| **What did they say?** | |
| **What lessons do we learn from them?** | |

Ask another group to tell the events of Jesus' birth.

## At Christmas we celebrate the Incarnation.

Christmas is a celebration of the Incarnation, the Son of God becoming man in the person of Jesus Christ. We recall the events of the Nativity, Jesus' birth.

The birth of Jesus took place in a stable. The Gospel tells us that animals were standing near the manger where the baby Jesus was laid. The child slept quietly in the night. Yet that is not why Christmas is a season of peace.

Christmas is a season of peace because Jesus is the Prince of Peace. Jesus shows us the way to peace with God and peace with one another. Jesus is the fulfillment of the promise announced by the prophet Isaiah: "A child is born . . . they name him . . . Prince of Peace" (Isaiah 9:5).

During his earthly life, Jesus told people about the Kingdom of God. The Kingdom of God is a kingdom of justice, love, and peace. Jesus called his followers to enter that kingdom and to become peacemakers, too.

It was not enough for Jesus himself to be peaceful. He also showed his disciples how to find peace in their hearts and how to build a more peaceful world.

Jesus taught us that the way to peace in our hearts is through prayer. We discover true peace by staying close to God. He also taught us to build peace in our world. We do this through acts of justice, mercy, and forgiveness.

Jesus came into our world at Christmas. He is our Savior who continues to show us the way to peace.

**Christmas**

## Did You Know?

**God shares his peace with us.**

## Activity

Christmas begins on December 25 but does not end until Epiphany on January 6. Write three ways you can celebrate the Christmas season. Be sure to include ways that you can share the peace of Christmas with those who are less fortunate. Share your favorite idea with the class.

_____

_____

_____

_____

# Christmas Prayer Ritual

 **"Joy to the World"**

**Leader:** Let us make the Sign of the Cross: In the name of the Father, and of the Son, and of the Holy Spirit. Amen.

Lord God, you sent your Son, Jesus, to be born of the Virgin Mary. He brings peace and joy into our hearts. Bless all of us who stand now to praise the newborn King. Let it remind us of how Jesus was born into the world and into our hearts.

Let us listen to the words of the prophet Isaiah, who speaks of the giving of good news from a mountaintop:

> "How beautiful upon the mountains
>   are the feet of the one bringing good news,
> Announcing peace, bearing good news,
>   announcing salvation, saying to Zion,
> 'Your God is King!'" (Isaiah 52:7).

We go to the mountains, the hills, and everywhere to raise our voices in praise to Jesus at his birth:

**All (sing):** Go tell it on the mountain, over the hill and everywhere.

Go tell it on the mountain, that Jesus Christ is born.

**Leader:** We sing from the mountaintop that Jesus brings joy into our hearts:

**All (sing):** Go tell it on the mountain, over the hill and everywhere.

Go tell it on the mountain, that Jesus Christ is born.

**Leader:** We sing from the mountaintop that Jesus brings peace into our hearts:

**All (sing):** Go tell it on the mountain, over the hill and everywhere.

Go tell it on the mountain, that Jesus Christ is born.

**Leader:** We sing from the mountaintop that Jesus brings love into our hearts:

**All (sing):** Go tell it on the mountain, over the hill and everywhere.

Go tell it on the mountain, that Jesus Christ is born.

**Leader:** We sing from the mountaintop that Jesus brings mercy into our lives:

**All (sing):** Go tell it on the mountain, over the hill and everywhere.

Go tell it on the mountain, that Jesus Christ is born.

**Leader:** We sing from the mountaintop that Jesus brings justice into the world:

**All (sing):** Go tell it on the mountain, over the hill and everywhere.

Go tell it on the mountain, that Jesus Christ is born.

**Leader:** May the peace that Jesus brings to the world be with you always.

**All:** And with your spirit!

**Leader:** Now offer each other a sign of peace.

(*All go around the room and offer a sign of peace to one another.*)

**Leader:** Go out into the world and share the peace of Christmas with everyone you meet!

**All (sing):** Go tell it on the mountain, over the hill and everywhere.

Go tell it on the mountain, that Jesus Christ is born.

What meaning does the birth of Jesus have in my life?

## Mini-Task

The Christmas season is a time of peace. We celebrate the birth of the one we call the Prince of Peace: Jesus. We work for peace in the world.

Recall what you have learned about the season of Christmas. Brainstorm ideas for service that young people could do inspired by Jesus as Light of the World and Prince of Peace. Record your best idea in the chart below.

| Christmas Service Ministry | |
| --- | --- |
| **Whom or what will this serve?** | |
| **What service will you provide?** | |
| **Where will you do the service?** | |
| **When will the service take place?** | |
| **Why is this service important?** | |
| **How does this service connect to Christmas?** | |

Discuss your idea with a partner. Share suggestions for ways your idea could be put into action.

**Want to do more? Go to your Portfolio to continue this activity.**

# At Home

Talk with your family about ways you can build a more peaceful world. Choose something to do this week.

How are we called to
repentance today?

**Lesson 24**

Lent

*"Christ Jesus came into the world to save sinners . . . Christ Jesus might display all his patience as an example for those who would come to believe in him for everlasting life."*

*1 Timothy 1:15–16*

# Gathering Prayer

**Leader:** Let us open our hearts and pray for everyone this Lent. We ask the Lord to help us live as he has shown us and love as he has loved us.

This Lent, we pray for the leaders of the world, that they will be an example of Christ's love to their people.

**All:** O Lord, we lift our prayers to you.

**Leader:** This Lent, we pray for the pope, bishops, priests, religious, and lay leaders of the Church as they share the love of Christ with all of us.

**All:** O Lord, we lift our prayers to you.

**Leader:** This Lent, we pray for all those who are sick, lonely, depressed, grieving, and hurting in any way.

**All:** O Lord, we lift our prayers to you.

**Leader:** We pray for all those who have died, recently or at any time (*pause*). For all of these, we pray:

**All:** O Lord, we lift our prayers to you.

**Leader:** This Lent, help us to pray more deeply together at Mass each weekend.

**All:** O Lord, we lift our prayers to you.

## Activity

Lent is a time of year when we turn from sin and become closer to God. One way we can prepare for Lent is to assemble a spiritual bouquet of prayers and devotions as an offering to Mary and Jesus. Make your own spiritual bouquet for this Lent. Add your ideas to the list.

• Pray the rosary

• Visit the Blessed Sacrament

• _____

• _____

Choose one of your ideas to add to a class bouquet on the whiteboard.

## Lent calls us to renewal.

Lent is a time of conversion. We turn away from sin and turn back to God, the source of all life and goodness. Conversion is the way to happiness because true joy is found in being close to God.

The season of Lent invites us to pray often. We can pray wherever we are, alone or with others, aloud or silently. God our loving Father always hears our prayers. The most important prayer that the Church prays together is the Mass. We may pray in our own words or simply be quiet and peaceful in his presence.

How do we turn away from sin? We listen to God's Word and the inner voice of our conscience and choose to do what is good. Just and loving actions are a sign that we are turning from sin. Each time we choose to do what is good, it is a step on the road to conversion. Jesus teaches us to forgive one another and to build bridges of reconciliation. This is part of conversion, too.

Lent is a time to show special concern for the poor and needy. Whenever we help the poor, we are fulfilling the command of Jesus to love one another as he has loved us. One way to help the poor is by giving alms, usually in the form of financial support. Lent is also a time for fasting. When we fast, we "give something up." This could be candy, video games, television, or other

Lent

things we enjoy but do not need. The purpose of fasting is to rediscover our dependence on God. The work of conversion takes time and effort. The good news is that we do not have to rely on our efforts alone. The Holy Spirit helps us. During Lent, the work of conversion prepares us to renew our baptismal promises at Easter.

## Did You Know?

**It is important to reflect on our lives.**

## Activity

Work in small groups to think of a situation in which young people might be tempted to do the wrong thing. Write two or three good or loving actions young people can do to turn away from sin.

_____

_____

_____

# Readers Theater

## Jesus' Temptation in the Desert

(Based on Matthew 4:1–11; Luke 4:1–13)

### Roles: Narrator 1, Narrator 2, Narrator 3, Jesus

*Satan tried to tempt Jesus three times,
but Jesus would not be moved.*

**Narrator 1:** After John the Baptist baptized Jesus, Jesus returned from the Jordan River and was filled with the Holy Spirit.

**Narrator 2:** Jesus was led by the Spirit into the desert for forty days and forty nights.

**Narrator 3:** It was there in the desert that Jesus would be tempted by the Devil.

**Narrator 1:** During those forty days and forty nights, Jesus ate nothing. At the end of this time, he was very hungry. The Devil approached Jesus and tempted him. He said to him: "If you are the Son of God, command that these stones become loaves of bread" (Matthew 4:3).

**Jesus:** "It is written:
　　'One does not live by bread alone,
　　　but by every word that comes forth from the mouth of God'"
(Matthew 4:4).

**Narrator 2:** Then the Devil took Jesus to the holy city and made him stand on the highest wall in the Temple. Looking down at the dizzying height, the Devil tempted Jesus. He challenged Jesus to throw himself down, saying: "If you are the Son of God, throw yourself down. For it is written:
　　'He will command his angels concerning you'
　　　and 'with their hands they will support you,
　　lest you dash your foot against a stone'" (Matthew 4:6).

**Jesus:** "Again it is written, 'You shall not put the Lord, your God, to the test'" (Matthew 4:7).

**Narrator 3:** The Devil took Jesus way up to a very high mountain. There, the Devil showed Jesus all the magnificent kingdoms in the world. The Devil again tempted Jesus, saying: "All these I shall give to you, if you will prostrate yourself and worship me" (Matthew 4:9).

**Jesus:** "Get away, Satan! It is written:
'The Lord, your God, shall you worship
and him alone shall you serve'" (Matthew 4:10).

**Narrator 1:** The Devil ended all the temptations and left Jesus. Angels surrounded Jesus and comforted him.

## How can I turn away from sin?

## Mini-Task

Lent is a time when we experience conversion as we turn away from sin and toward God. It is a time of prayer, penance (fasting), and good works (almsgiving). We remember the sacrifice Jesus has made for us.

Use what you have learned about the season of Lent as you brainstorm ideas for service that young people could do during Lent.

Record your best idea in the chart below.

| Lent Service Ministry | |
|---|---|
| **Whom or what will this serve?** | |
| **What service will you provide?** | |
| **Where will you do the service?** | |
| **When will the service take place?** | |
| **Why is this service important?** | |
| **How does this service connect to Lent?** | |

Discuss your idea with a partner. Share suggestions for ways your idea could be put into action.

 **Want to do more? Go to your Portfolio to continue this activity.**

# At Home

Pray together as a family. Ask God to help your family avoid temptation, experience conversion, and choose what is good.

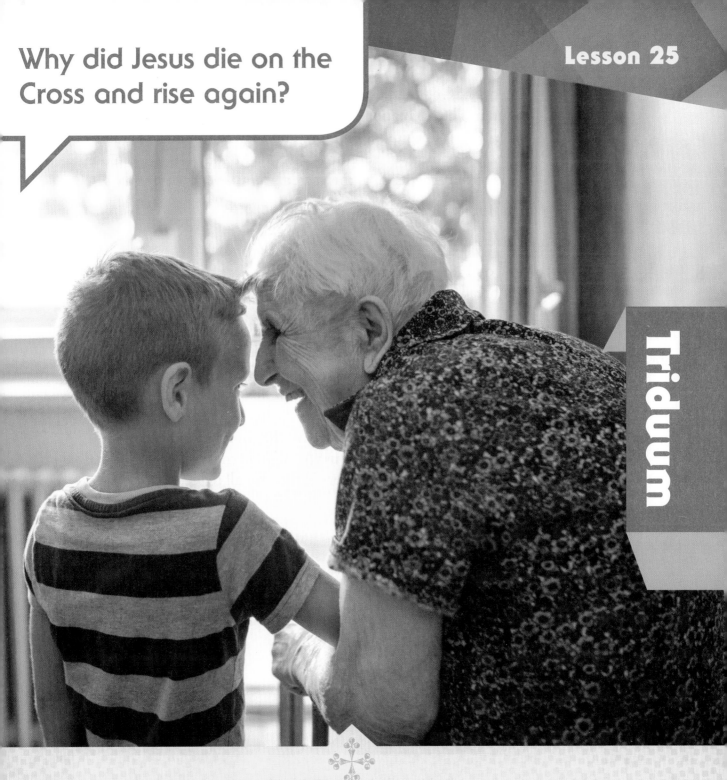

Why did Jesus die on the Cross and rise again?

Triduum

*"I have given you a model to follow, so that as I have done for you, you should also do."*

*John 13:15*

# Gathering Prayer

**Leader:** The love of God that Jesus has shown us is celebrated during the Triduum. The celebration of the Triduum is one liturgy that happens over three days, beginning on Holy Thursday, continuing on Good Friday, and ending with evening prayer on Sunday. Let us open our hearts to the experience of this sacred liturgy over the three days.

Jesus, forever I will sing of your love.

**All:** Forever I will sing of your love.

**Leader:** Jesus, on Holy Thursday, as we commemorate the Last Supper, you took bread and wine and shared it, giving us your Body and Blood.

**All:** Forever I will sing of your love.

**Leader:** Jesus, on Good Friday, we gather to hear of your Passion and Death on the Cross. Your outstretched hands open to us all.

**All:** Forever I will sing of your love.

**Leader:** Jesus, in the Easter liturgies, we give thanks for your love for us. You conquered death, leaving us your light in the form of the Paschal candle, shining brightly in every church for all to see.

**All:** Forever I will sing of your love.

**Leader:** Jesus, forever I will sing of your love.

**All:** Forever I will sing of your love.

## Activity

The Friday that Jesus died is called Good Friday. It might seem strange to call such a sad day "good." Yet, think about all the good things that happened for us on this day. Share your thoughts with your group.

For _____, we thank you, Jesus.

Make a list of everyone's ideas to add to a group prayer of thanksgiving.

**The Triduum is the high point of the liturgical year.**

On the night before Jesus died, he knew that he would no longer be present to his closest followers as he had been before. On that last night, Jesus shared his last Passover meal with them. He prayed for his followers and showed them two ways they could always remember him.

The first was the meal itself. He broke bread and gave it to them, saying "This is my Body." He shared a cup of wine with them, saying "This is my Blood." This was the first Eucharist. The bread and wine became Jesus' true Body and Blood. Whenever his followers did this in remembrance of him, Jesus was really present. The wine and the bread became his Body and Blood. This is what we celebrate at every Mass.

The second way his followers could remember Jesus was through acts of humble service. Jesus gave them an example of service by washing their feet. This was something that only a servant would do. Jesus told his followers that

they should follow his example and serve others humbly.

Today the Church remembers Jesus in the Eucharist and by following his example of service. We remember and give thanks for these things in the liturgy of Holy Thursday. They are part of the Paschal Mystery of Christ's Death and Resurrection, celebrated during the Triduum.

## Did You Know?

 **We are called to serve.**

## Activity

The Stations of the Cross devotion (see page 247 in your book) recalls the events of Jesus' Passion and Death, from the time he was condemned to death until he was buried. Visit your parish church to pray the stations as a group, or pray "By your holy Cross, you have redeemed the world" after your catechist reads the name of each station.

# Readers Theater

## Agony in the Garden

(Based on Matthew 26:36–46)

### Roles: Narrator 1, Narrator 2, Narrator 3, Jesus

*Jesus prays to his Father in the Garden of Gethsemane
while his disciples wait, asleep.*

**Narrator 1:** It was the night when Jesus broke bread with his disciples and two days before he was to be crucified. After walking for a time, Jesus and his disciples arrived at a city garden at the foot of the Mount of Olives in Jerusalem—a place called Gethsemane. Jesus spoke to them:

**Jesus:** "Sit here while I go over there and pray" (Matthew 26:36).

**Narrator 2:** Jesus went into the garden with Peter and the two sons of a disciple called Zebedee. Immediately, Jesus began to feel great sorrow and suffering. Jesus addressed the three.

**Jesus:** "My soul is sorrowful even to death. Remain here and keep watch with me" (Matthew 26:38).

**Narrator 1:** Jesus walked a little further into the garden when suddenly he collapsed and fell to the ground, praying.

**Jesus:** "My Father, if it is possible, let this cup pass from me; yet, not as I will, but as you will" (Matthew 26:39).

**Narrator 3:** Jesus then returned to his disciples. They all had fallen asleep. Jesus spoke to Peter.

**Jesus:** "So you could not keep watch with me for one hour?
Watch and pray that you may not undergo the test.
The spirit is willing, but the flesh is weak" (Matthew 26:40–41).

**Narrator 1:** Jesus then returned to the garden for a second time. Here he prayed:

**Jesus:** "My Father, if it is not possible that this cup pass without my drinking it, your will be done!" (Matthew 26:42).

**Narrator 2:** Jesus returned to his disciples. And once again, he found them sound asleep! Jesus left them for a third time and returned to the garden to pray again.

**Jesus:** "My Father, if it is not possible that this cup pass without my drinking it, your will be done!" (Matthew 26:42).

**Narrator 3:** Then Jesus returned for the last time to his disciples. He looked down at them and said:

**Jesus:** "Are you still sleeping and taking your rest? Behold, the hour is at hand when the Son of Man is to be handed over to sinners. Get up, let us go. Look, my betrayer is at hand" (Matthew 26:45–46).

**Narrator 1:** At that moment, Judas arrived with a large, angry crowd.

Why did Jesus die on the Cross and rise again?

## Mini-Task

During the three solemn days of the Triduum, we remember Jesus' Passion, Death, and Resurrection. We remember the institution of the Eucharist and the washing of the disciples' feet on Holy Thursday, the events of the Passion on Good Friday, and Christ's glorious Resurrection on Holy Saturday at the Easter Vigil.

Use what you have learned about the season of the Triduum as you brainstorm ideas for service that young people could do to commemorate the three days. Record your best idea in the chart below.

| Triduum Service Ministry | |
| --- | --- |
| **Whom or what will you serve?** | |
| **What service will you provide?** | |
| **Where will you do the service?** | |
| **When will the service take place?** | |
| **Why is this service important?** | |
| **How does this service connect to the Triduum?** | |

Discuss your idea with a partner. Share suggestions for ways your idea could be put into action.

 **Want to do more? Go to your Portfolio to continue this activity.**

## At Home

Talk with your family about what humble service means to you. Choose something each member of your family can do as an act of service.

How is the Risen Jesus present in his Church?

Easter

"God raised him from the dead;
of this we are witnesses."

Acts of the Apostles 3:15

# Gathering Prayer

**Leader:** This is the season that we celebrate the Resurrection of our Lord, Jesus Christ. As people who now walk in the light of the Risen Christ, we are a living sign of Christ alive! Alleluia, alleluia, Christ is risen!

**All:** Alleluia, alleluia, Christ is risen!

**Leader:** The light of Christ has shattered the darkness of evil and sin. Alleluia, alleluia, Christ is risen!

**All:** Alleluia, alleluia, Christ is risen!

**Leader:** Let the joy of the Risen Christ be known throughout the world! Alleluia, alleluia, Christ is risen!

**All:** Alleluia, alleluia, Christ is risen!

**Leader:** Father, you sent us your Son, Jesus, to save us. Through his Death and Resurrection, he has conquered sin and death. Your love for us is so amazing! Alleluia, alleluia, Christ is risen!

**All:** Alleluia, alleluia, Christ is risen!

**Leader:** Risen Christ, our hearts are filled with the joy of Easter! Alleluia, alleluia, Christ is risen!

**All:** Alleluia, alleluia, Christ is risen.

## Activity

How are each of these items a sign of the new life of Christ at Easter?

Share your ideas with your group.

## Easter celebrates the new life of Christ's Resurrection.

Saint Paul tells us that Christ's Resurrection gives us the power to "live in newness of life" (Romans 6:4). We receive this gift through Baptism.

The Easter season is a time to remember our Baptism. We renew our commitment to walk in "newness of life." The Church celebrates Baptism at Easter. All the faithful renew their baptismal promises during Easter, too.

In some churches, the baptismal font is beautifully decorated throughout the Easter season. Some parishes also use the Sprinkling Rite at Mass during the Easter season as a reminder of Baptism. The priest walks through the church and sprinkles the assembly with holy water from a special container called an *aspergillum*. At Easter, the newly baptized receive the light of Christ from the Paschal candle. The candle remains lighted in our churches through the whole season.

The season is a time for the assembly to welcome everyone who celebrates the Sacraments of Initiation at Easter. They are now members of our family of faith. Together we share in works of charity in our parish, school, and neighborhood.

Jesus prayed for his disciples, that "they may all be one" (John 17:21). When we build up the community of faith, we cooperate with God's grace and respond to the prayer of Jesus.

## Did You Know?

 **We renew life every day.**

Easter

## Activity

The week after Easter is called the octave of Easter. The Church asks us to celebrate each day by remembering the Resurrection for eight days. Fill in the chart with something you could do each day to make the octave special.

| Easter | Monday | Tuesday | Wednesday | Thursday | Friday | Saturday |
|--------|--------|---------|-----------|----------|--------|----------|
|        |        |         |           |          |        |          |

# Easter Prayer Ritual

 **"Sing to the Mountains,"** Bob Dufford, SJ/OCP

**Leader:** In the name of the Father, and of the Son, and of the Holy Spirit. Amen.

Easter is not just a day but a long feast ending on and including the great feast of Pentecost. The Church celebrates the season of Easter for fifty days! The events that took place after the Resurrection that we hear about in the Scripture readings at Mass are some of the most powerful accounts of our faith.

Listen now to this account from the Gospel of John (15:1–5, 8):

**Reader:** Jesus said to his disciples: "I am the true vine, and my Father is the vine grower. He takes away every branch in me that does not bear fruit, and every one that does he prunes so that it bears more fruit. You are already pruned because of the word that I spoke to you. Remain in me, as I remain in you. Just as a branch cannot bear fruit on its own unless it remains on the vine, so neither can you unless you remain in me. I am the vine, you are the branches. Whoever remains in me and I in him will bear much fruit, because without me you can do nothing. . . . By this is my Father glorified, that you bear much fruit and become my disciples."

**Leader:** Let us take a few minutes to think about this reading by imagining that you are a branch on a vine in a garden. What images do you see? Imagine that the vine is Jesus and you are a branch of his vine. How does that make you feel?

When we are connected to Jesus, we can do anything. We become the eyes and hands of Christ. As we pray, let us join our hands as a living sign that we are the Body of Christ in the world.

**All:** We are the eyes and hands of Christ.

**Leader:** When we live as followers of Christ, we become disciples.

**All:** We are the eyes and hands of Christ.

**Leader:** When we are gathered with others at Mass, Jesus is with us.

**All:** We are the eyes and hands of Christ.

**Leader:** When we act as one in Christ with others, we become the Body of Christ.

**All:** We are the eyes and hands of Christ.

**Leader:** Let us sing "Sing to the Mountains."

## Mini-Task

Easter is a time when we celebrate the Risen Christ and remember his Resurrection. We welcome the newly baptized into our parish family and celebrate with them.

Review what you have learned about the season of Easter to brainstorm ideas for service that young people could do to commemorate the Easter season. Record your best idea in the chart below.

| Easter Service Ministry | |
| --- | --- |
| **Whom or what will you serve?** | |
| **What service will you provide?** | |
| **Where will you do the service?** | |
| **When will the service take place?** | |
| **Why is this service important?** | |
| **How does this service connect to Easter?** | |

Discuss your idea with a partner. Share suggestions for ways your idea could be put into action.

 **Want to do more? Go to your Portfolio to continue this activity.**

 **At Home**

As a family, pray for those who have recently joined your parish. Let these people know you are praying for them next Sunday at Mass.

Who is the Holy Spirit?

Pentecost

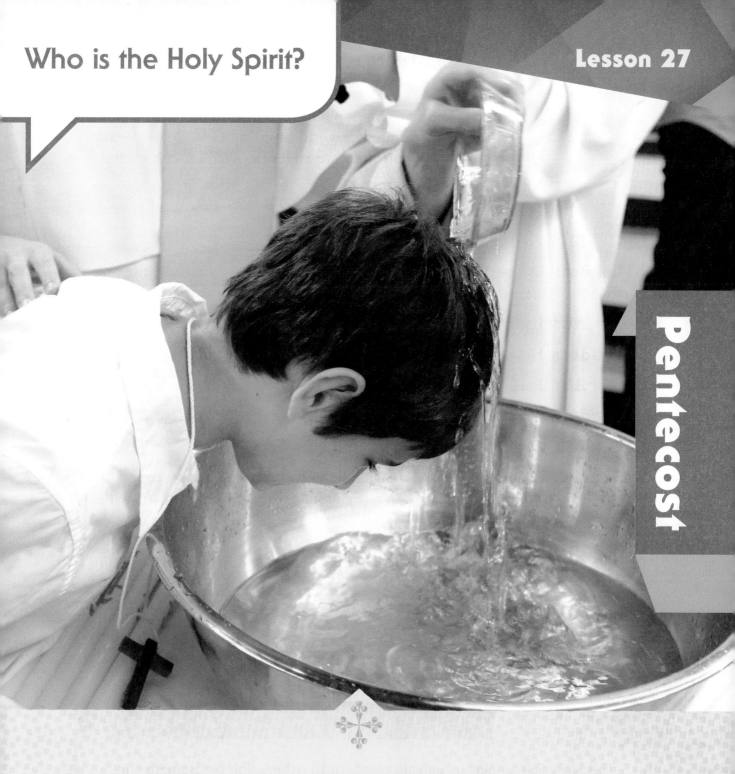

*"Repent and be baptized, every one of you, in the name of Jesus Christ for the forgiveness of your sins; and you will receive the gift of the holy Spirit."*

Acts of the Apostles 2:38

# Gathering Prayer

**Leader:** The great feast of Pentecost is sometimes called the "birthday" of the Church. The living Spirit of God came down on the disciples and sent them forth into the world to spread God's love. We ask God to send us his Spirit that we might be disciples, celebrating Christ within us.

Lord, send us your Spirit.

**All:** Lord, send us your Spirit.

**Leader:** O God, we thank you for sending us the gifts of your Spirit so that we, too, can be a witness of your love.

**All:** Lord, send us your Spirit.

**Leader:** Holy Spirit, dwell in us. Fill us with the fire of your love.

**All:** Lord, send us your Spirit.

**Leader:** Holy Spirit, guide our lives to follow in the steps of Jesus.

**All:** Lord, send us your Spirit.

**Leader:** Come, Holy Spirit, come. Fill our hearts with your peace and love, that we might share the love of Christ that is in our hearts with everyone we meet.

**All:** Lord, send us your Spirit.

## Activity

The Holy Spirit helps us explain our faith to others. Tell a classmate why you believe in Jesus. Let him or her ask you questions about your faith. Then trade places. Here are some questions you might ask:

Who first taught you about Jesus?

What is your favorite thing about Jesus?

How does Jesus help you?

Be sure to listen respectfully when it is your turn to do so.

## The Holy Spirit guides the Church.

Pentecost Sunday, fifty days after Easter, is a celebration of the coming of the Holy Spirit. The liturgical color of Pentecost is red. There is a special hymn we sing called the Sequence. It expresses the confident hope that the Holy Spirit will come to the Church today.

On Pentecost, we remember how the Holy Spirit changed the Apostles from timid followers into bold witnesses. Through the power of the Holy Spirit, the Apostles of the Church went out to proclaim that Jesus is Lord. Many people believed in their message, and the Church grew in numbers and in faith.

The Holy Spirit still builds up and holds the Church together to carry on the mission of Jesus. The Spirit is active between people and within each one of us as well. The Holy Spirit dwells in our hearts, filling us with joy and hope and helping us to pray. We can pray to the Holy Spirit for guidance, strength, and wisdom.

We know that the Holy Spirit dwells within us when we see the fruits of the Spirit in the way that we live. When we celebrate Pentecost, we are grateful for the Holy Spirit!

## Did You Know?

**You have an important message to share.**

## Activity

How can you tell if the Holy Spirit is active in someone's life? Name some of the qualities, or fruits, of the Holy Spirit that such a person would show.

- patience
- generosity
- _____

- _____
- _____
- _____

# Pentecost Prayer Ritual

 **"Lord, Send Out Your Spirit,"** Craig Colson/OCP

**Leader:** The great feast of Pentecost is the end of the Easter season. We celebrate the event in which God the Holy Spirit came into the lives of the Apostles, who were then sent out into the world to teach about Jesus.

Let us listen to the description of the first Pentecost (Acts of the Apostles 2:1–4):

**Reader:** "When the time for Pentecost was fulfilled, they were all in one place together. And suddenly there came from the sky a noise like a strong driving wind, and it filled the entire house in which they were. Then there appeared to them tongues as of fire, which parted and came to rest on each one of them. And they were all filled with the Holy Spirit and began to speak in different tongues, as the Spirit enabled them to proclaim."

**Leader:** Let us take a few minutes to reflect on the reading that we just heard.

*(Silent reflection)*

**Leader:** What do you think it would have been like to be in a house that was suddenly filled with wind? What do you think it would have been like to suddenly have tongues of fire on each of your heads, and then to suddenly be able to speak in many different languages? Is there anything in our lives that would be like this experience?

**Leader:** Let us pray:

At our Baptism, we are blessed with water and given the light of Christ to follow. The Holy Spirit came upon us that we might grow and be a disciple of Christ, and to act as Christ in the world. The Spirit of God is upon us. We are anointed to spread the Good News.

**All:** We are anointed to spread the Good News.

**Leader:** We are called to bring comfort to those who are hurting.

**All:** We are anointed to spread the Good News.

**Leader:** We are called to lift up those who reach out to us.

**All:** We are anointed to spread the Good News.

**Leader:** We are called to be light in a darkened world.

**All:** We are anointed to spread the Good News.

**Leader:** We are called to live as Christ is alive in us.

**All:** We are anointed to spread the Good News.

**Leader:** We will now come forward to bless ourselves with water and listen to the song "Lord, Send Out Your Spirit."

*(Listen to the song.)*

**Leader:** Let us sing the song "Lord, Send Out Your Spirit."

*(All sing.)*

**Leader:** We will close this Prayer Ritual by offering one another a sign of peace.

## Mini-Task

Pentecost is a time when we celebrate the beginning of the work of the Church. We remember the Holy Spirit's coming to the Apostles and Mary after Jesus had ascended to God the Father in heaven.

Review what you have learned about the feast of Pentecost to brainstorm ideas for service that young people could do to commemorate Pentecost. Record your best idea in the chart below.

| Pentecost Service Ministry | |
|---|---|
| **Whom or what will you serve?** | |
| **What service will you provide?** | |
| **Where will you do the service?** | |
| **When will the service take place?** | |
| **Why is this service important?** | |
| **How does this service connect to Pentecost?** | |

Discuss your idea with a partner. Share suggestions for ways your idea could be put into action.

 **Want to do more? Go to your Portfolio to continue this activity.**

# At Home

Talk with your family about ways that the Holy Spirit dwells in you. Together, pray to the Holy Spirit asking him to guide you in your life of Christian discipleship.

How do we grow as Jesus' followers?

Ordinary Time

*"Live in a manner worthy of the Lord, so as to be fully pleasing, in every good work bearing fruit and growing in the knowledge of God."*

*Colossians 1:10*

# Gathering Prayer

**Leader:** Let us pray during Ordinary Time that the mission of Jesus may be born in our own hearts. We ask Jesus to make us his disciples, that we follow his teachings and bring the Good News to everyone!

Lord Jesus, help us to be your disciples.

**All:** Lord Jesus, help us to be your disciples.

**Leader:** In our daily lives with our families:

**All:** Lord Jesus, help us to be your disciples.

**Leader:** In our schools with our friends and all students and teachers:

**All:** Lord Jesus, help us to be your disciples.

**Leader:** In our neighborhoods and in all other activities:

**All:** Lord Jesus, help us to be your disciples.

**Leader:** When we go to Mass with our families:

**All:** Lord Jesus, help us to be your disciples.

**Leader:** When we see someone alone, sad, or afraid;

**All:** Lord Jesus, help us to be your disciples.

**Leader:** Lord Jesus, help us to be your disciples.

**All:** Lord Jesus, help us to be your disciples.

## Activity

Most of the Church year happens during the season of Ordinary Time. But *ordinary* does not mean dull or boring. We call the season Ordinary Time because the weeks of the season are numbered, or counted, with the ordinal numbers—1, 2, 3, and so on. Ordinary Time begins the day after the Feast of the Epiphany, or Monday of the First Week. The following Sunday is the Second Sunday in Ordinary Time, and so on. Work with a partner to look at a liturgical calendar. Count how many Sundays are part of Ordinary Time. Then talk as a group about ways we can be Jesus' disciples every week of this season.

## The Church celebrates Jesus' life and teachings.

Ordinary Time is the longest season in the liturgical calendar. It begins after the Christmas season and continues for several weeks, until Lent begins. After Pentecost Sunday, Ordinary Time starts again and continues until the end of the liturgical year. There are thirty-three or thirty-four Sundays in Ordinary Time.

During Ordinary Time, the Church celebrates on the life of Jesus Christ. We listen to his teachings and try to act as he did. We are challenged to follow the way of Christ through the readings at Mass.

The readings follow a three-year cycle. In Year A, we hear readings from the Gospel of Matthew. In Year B, we hear readings from the Gospel of Mark and some from the Gospel of John. In Year C, we hear the Gospel of Luke.

Each of the evangelists presents the narrative of Jesus' life and ministry in his own way. In any given year, we can follow the path of Jesus through the eyes of a particular Gospel writer. We take a fresh look at Jesus and his mission. We grow in holiness day by day and walk with Christ.

## Did You Know?

**Now is a time to be holy.**

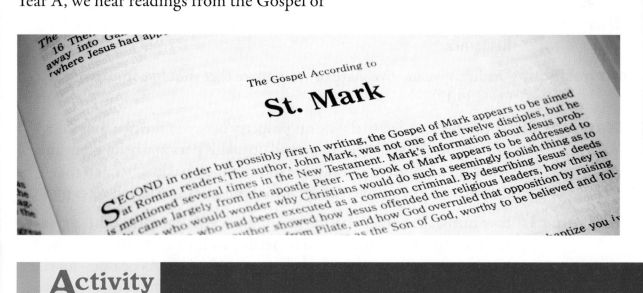

The Gospel According to

### St. Mark

SECOND in order but possibly first in writing, the Gospel of Mark appears to be aimed at Roman readers. The author, John Mark, was not one of the twelve disciples, but he is mentioned several times in the New Testament. Mark's information about Jesus probably came largely from the apostle Peter. The book of Mark appears to be addressed to who would wonder why Christians would do such a seemingly foolish thing as to who had been executed as a common criminal. By describing Jesus' deeds author showed how Jesus offended the religious leaders, how they in from Pilate, and how God overruled that opposition by raising as the Son of God, worthy to be believed and fol-

## Activity

The evangelists and other holy people did extraordinary things. Yet they had to do "ordinary" things, too, such as eat and sleep. We can all grow in holiness every day by doing ordinary things. Brainstorm with a friend about ways that you can use these activities to honor God.

Doing chores: _____

Playing sports: _____

Going to school: _____

Doing homework: _____

Eating a meal: _____

# Readers Theater

## The Parable of the Lost Son

(Based on Luke 15:11–32)

### Roles: Narrator 1, Narrator 2, Narrator 3, Father, Younger Son

*Jesus tells his followers about God's love through a parable.*

**Narrator 1:** Parables are simple stories used to explain a moral or spiritual lesson. In the Parable of the Lost Son, Jesus shows us God's great love for the sinner who is genuinely sorry for sinning against God.

**Narrator 2:** There was a man who had two sons. The younger son spoke to his father.

**Younger Son:** "Father, give me the share of your estate that should come to me" (Luke 15:12).

**Narrator 3:** The father decided to divide his property between the two sons. In a little while, the younger son packed up all his personal belongings and set off to a country far away. He did not look back. There, in that distant land, the young man spent all his money on sin and corruption.

**Narrator 1:** Eventually, the young man ran out of money. At the same time, a great famine spread over the land. He needed to find a way to eat. So he hired himself out to a farm to help tend to the pigs. As he cared for the animals, he looked at their food with longing. But nobody gave him any food at all. It was then that he realized what a mistake he had made. He needed to ask forgiveness from his father.

**Narrator 2:** The younger son began his journey home. While he was still far away, his father caught sight of him and ran to him and hugged him tightly. His son spoke to him.

**Younger Son:** "Father, I have sinned against heaven and against you; I no longer deserve to be called your son" (Luke 15:21).

**Narrator 3:** But his father told his servants to prepare food for a special celebration and to clothe his son in the finest garments.

**Narrator 1:** While all this was happening, the older son had been out in the fields, working hard as he always had. As he neared the house, he heard the sounds of music and laughter. Surprised, he asked one of the servants what the celebration was about. The servant replied that his younger brother had returned safe and sound and his father had ordered a special feast to celebrate.

**Narrator 2:** The older brother was angry. He refused to enter the house. As his father pleaded with him to join the celebration, the older son angrily replied that he had worked all these years, serving his father, and never once did he get a special celebration in his honor.

**Narrator 3:** His father looked at his older son lovingly.

**Father:** "My son, you are here with me always; everything I have is yours. But now we must celebrate and rejoice, because your brother was dead and has come to life again; he was lost and has been found" (Luke 15:31–32).

How do we grow as Jesus' followers?

## Mini-Task

In Ordinary Time, we celebrate the public ministry of Jesus. We remember his care for all people and how much he especially loved children.

Review what you have learned about Ordinary Time to brainstorm ideas for service that young people could do during Ordinary Time. Record your best idea in the chart below.

| Ordinary Time Ministry | |
|---|---|
| **Whom or what will you serve?** | |
| **What service will you provide?** | |
| **Where will you do the service?** | |
| **When will the service take place?** | |
| **Why is this service important?** | |
| **How does this service connect to Ordinary Time?** | |

Discuss your idea with a partner. Share suggestions for ways your idea could be put into action.

 **Want to do more? Go to your Portfolio to continue this activity.**

Is there a book your family has read together often? What makes you want to read that book over and over again? Talk as a family about ways that we remember and learn new things from the readings at Mass.

# Welcome

## to your *Christ In Us* Sourcebook

## Our Father

Our Father, who art in heaven,
hallowed be thy name;
thy kingdom come;
thy will be done on earth as
    it is in heaven.
Give us this day our daily bread;
and forgive us our trespasses
as we forgive those who
    trespass against us;
and lead us not into
temptation,
but deliver us from evil.
Amen.

## Act of Contrition

My God,
I am sorry for my sins with
    all my heart.
In choosing to do wrong
and failing to do good,
I have sinned against you
whom I should love above
    all things.
I firmly intend, with your help,
to do penance,
to sin no more,
and to avoid whatever
    leads me to sin.
Our Savior Jesus Christ
suffered and died for us.
In his name, my God,
    have mercy.
Amen.

## Glory Be to the Father

Glory be to the Father
and to the Son
and to the Holy Spirit,
as it was in the beginning
is now, and ever shall be
world without end.
Amen.

## Apostles' Creed

I believe in God, the Father almighty,
    Creator of heaven and earth,
and in Jesus Christ, his only Son,
    our Lord,
who was conceived by the Holy Spirit,
born of the Virgin Mary,
suffered under Pontius Pilate,
was crucified, died and was buried;
he descended into hell;
on the third day he rose again
from the dead;
he ascended into heaven,
and is seated at the right hand
    of God the Father almighty;
from there he will come to judge
    the living and the dead.
I believe in the Holy Spirit,
    the holy catholic Church,
    the communion of saints,
    the forgiveness of sins,
    the resurrection of the body,
    and life everlasting. Amen.

## Hail Mary

Hail Mary, full of grace,
the Lord is with you!
Blessed are you among women,
and blessed is the fruit of
    your womb, Jesus.
Holy Mary, Mother of God,
pray for us sinners,
now and at the hour of our death.
Amen.

## Prayer to the Holy Spirit

Come, Holy Spirit, fill the hearts of your
    faithful.
And kindle in them the fire of your love.

Send forth your Spirit and they
    shall be created.
And you will renew the face of the earth.

## Morning Offering

O Jesus, I offer you all my prayers, works,
and sufferings of this day for all the
intentions of your most Sacred Heart.
Amen.

## Evening Prayer

Dear God, before I sleep
I want to thank you for this day,
so full of your kindness
and your joy.
I close my eyes to rest
safe in your loving care.

## Act of Faith

O God, we believe in all that Jesus has
taught us about you. We place all our trust
in you because of your great love for us.

## Act of Hope

O God, we never give up on your love.
We have hope and will work for your
kingdom to come and for a life that lasts
forever with you in heaven.

## Act of Love

O God, we love you above all things.
Help us to love ourselves and one another
as Jesus taught us to do.

### Prayer for Peace
(Prayer of Saint Francis)

Lord, make me an instrument of
    your peace:
where there is hatred, let me sow love;
where there is injury, pardon;
where there is doubt, faith;
where there is despair, hope;
where there is darkness, light;
where there is sadness, joy.

O divine Master, grant that I may not so
    much seek
to be consoled as to console,
to be understood as to understand,
to be loved as to love.
For it is in giving that we receive,
it is in pardoning that we are pardoned,
it is in dying that we are born to
    eternal life.

### Hail, Holy Queen

Hail, holy Queen, mother of mercy,
hail, our life, our sweetness, and
    our hope.
To you we cry, the children of Eve;
to you we send up our sighs,
mourning and weeping in this land
    of exile.
Turn, then, most gracious advocate,
your eyes of mercy toward us;
lead us home at last and show us
the blessed fruit of your womb,
Jesus: O clement, O loving, O sweet
    Virgin Mary.

### Prayer Before the Blessed Sacrament

Jesus,
you are God-with-us,
especially in this sacrament
of the Eucharist.
You love me as I am
and help me grow.

Come and be with me
in all my joys and sorrows.
Help me share your peace and love
with everyone I meet.
I ask in your name. Amen.

# How to Pray the Rosary

A rosary is made up of groups of beads arranged in a circle. It begins with a cross followed by one large bead and three small ones. The next large bead (just before the medal) begins the first "decade." Each decade consists of one large bead followed by ten smaller beads.

Begin to pray the Rosary with the Sign of the Cross. Recite the Apostles' Creed. Then pray one Our Father, three Hail Marys, and one Glory Be to the Father.

To pray each decade, say an Our Father on the large bead and a Hail Mary on each of the ten smaller beads. Close each decade by praying the Glory Be to the Father. Pray the Hail, Holy Queen as the last prayer of the Rosary.

The mysteries of the Rosary are special events in the lives of Jesus and Mary. As you pray each decade, think of the appropriate Joyful Mystery, Sorrowful Mystery, Glorious Mystery, or Mystery of Light.

## The Five Joyful Mysteries

1. The Annunciation
2. The Visitation
3. The Birth of Jesus
4. The Presentation of Jesus in the Temple
5. The Finding of Jesus in the Temple

## The Five Sorrowful Mysteries

1. The Agony in the Garden
2. The Scourging at the Pillar
3. The Crowning with Thorns
4. The Carrying of the Cross
5. The Crucifixion and Death of Jesus

## The Five Glorious Mysteries

1. The Resurrection
2. The Ascension
3. The Descent of the Holy Spirit upon the Apostles
4. The Assumption of Mary into Heaven
5. The Coronation of Mary as Queen of Heaven

## The Five Mysteries of Light

1. Jesus' Baptism in the Jordan
2. The Miracle at the Wedding at Cana
3. Jesus Announces the Kingdom of God
4. The Transfiguration
5. The Institution of the Eucharist

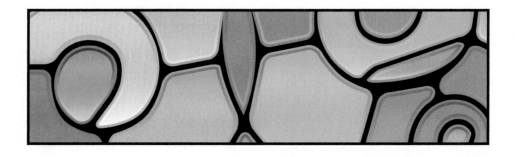

1 **sanctuary** the part of the church that includes the altar and the ambo. The word *sanctuary* means "holy place."

2 **altar** the special table that is the center of the celebration of the Liturgy of the Eucharist, also called the Table of the Lord.

3 **crucifix** a cross with a figure of Christ crucified, displayed in the sanctuary.

4 **tabernacle** the special place in the church in which the Most Blessed Sacrament is placed in reserve.

5 **sanctuary lamp** light or candle that is always lit near the tabernacle. It helps us to remember that Jesus is really present in the Most Blessed Sacrament.

6 **ambo** a sacred reading stand called the Table of the Word of God. The ambo is used only for proclamation of the Scripture in the liturgy.

7 **chalice** the special cup into which the priest pours grape wine that becomes the Blood of Christ during the Liturgy of the Eucharist.

8 **paten** the special plate on which the priest places the wheat bread that becomes the Body of Christ during the Liturgy of the Eucharist.

9 **cruets** small glass jars that contain the water and the grape wine used at Mass.

10 **presider's chair** chair on which the priest who is celebrating Mass sits.

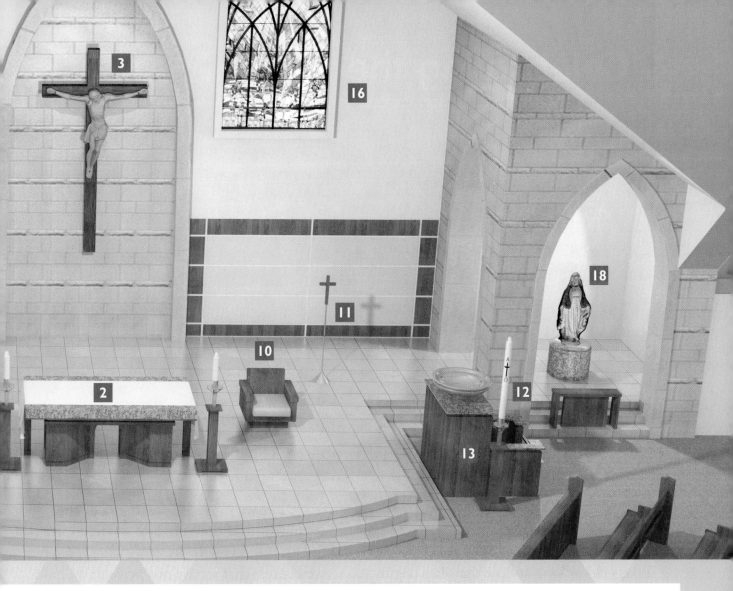

**11** **processional cross** cross with a figure of Christ crucified that is carried in the entrance procession and may also be carried during the offertory procession and during recessional.

**12** **Paschal candle** a large candle that is blessed and lit every Easter. The lighted Paschal candle represents the Risen Christ among us. The flame of the Paschal candle is used to light baptismal candles.

**13** **baptismal font or pool** contains the water that is blessed and used during the Sacrament of Baptism.

**14** **Stations of the Cross** fourteen pictures that help us to follow the footsteps of Jesus during his Passion and Death on the Cross.

**15** **Reconciliation room or confessional** a separate space for celebrating the Sacrament of Penance and Reconciliation. This is where you meet the priest for individual confession and absolution. You may sit and talk to him face-to-face or kneel behind a screen.

**16** **stained glass** colorful windows that may show saints or scenes from Scripture.

**17** **pews** where the assembly is seated during the celebration of Mass.

**18** **statue of Mary** image of the Mother of God, our greatest saint. Statues of other saints may also be found in the church.

# Celebrating the Mass

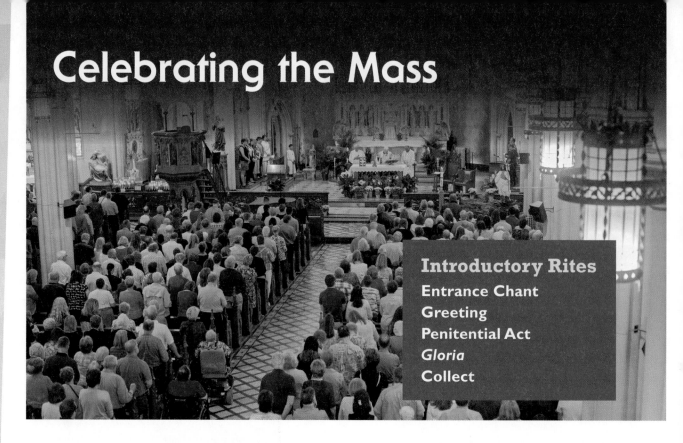

**Introductory Rites**
Entrance Chant
Greeting
Penitential Act
*Gloria*
Collect

Do you and your family sometimes wonder what the Mass is really all about? Here is a simple guide that brings awareness to the greatest prayer of the Catholic Church—the celebration of the Eucharist, or Mass.

Take a closer look at how the Mass begins and ends and at the two parts of the Mass: the Liturgy of the Word and the Liturgy of the Eucharist. All our prayers of praise and thanksgiving form one single act of worship. Share the meaning of these sacred moments with your family.

## We Gather . . .

What better way to begin our worship than with an entrance song and a procession of the priest and other ministers! This shows our unity, for together we are the Body of Christ—the Church—gathered in God's name. Watch as the priest and deacon kiss the altar and bow. It is on the altar, the table of the Lord, that the sacrifice of Christ is made present. We remember and make present the work of salvation accomplished by Jesus

through his life, Death, Resurrection, and Ascension into heaven.

Together we pray: "In the name of the Father, and of the Son, and of the Holy Spirit." God is with us. In God's presence, we confess that we are not perfect; we have sinned. We pray for God's mercy and ask for the prayers of the community and all the saints. In this way, we prepare ourselves—mind, heart, and soul—to participate in the sacred mysteries of the Mass.

On most Sundays we pray an ancient hymn called the *Gloria*, first sung by the angels at the birth of Christ: "Glory to God in the highest . . . /For you alone are the Lord, / you alone are the Most High, / Jesus Christ, / with the Holy Spirit, / in the glory of God the Father." This hymn of praise speaks of the mystery of the Trinity, the Triune God, in whose name we gather.

The priest then prays the Collect, the opening prayer that expresses the theme of the celebration and the needs and hopes of the assembly.

## Liturgy of the Word

God placed in each of our hearts a desire to know him better. At Mass we are invited to actively listen to the Word of God. In Scripture, God speaks to us of the wonders of salvation and of his love for all creation. Yet God also has a special message for each individual who hears his holy Word. What might that be for you or for members of your family?

Our response after listening to the First Reading, usually from the Old Testament, and the Second Reading, from the New Testament, is "Thanks be to God." God's Word is not merely a collection of past events. God continues to act in our lives today; his Word has the power to transform us.

Between these readings is the Responsorial Psalm, which can be spoken or sung. Jesus himself prayed the psalms, which express every kind of emotion as well as what we desire from God. The psalms are beloved prayers of the Bible in which we ask the Lord for many things, such as insight, renewal, guidance, strength, and protection.

Our dialogue with God continues as we prepare to encounter Christ in the Gospel.

Now, though, we are standing, singing *Alleluia* or other words of praise. Standing is a sign of honor for the Gospel, the Good News of Jesus Christ. This is the high point of the Liturgy of the Word. Jesus Christ, our Savior, speaks to us—comforting, strengthening, and calling us to live as his disciples. As the priest or deacon introduces the Gospel (Matthew, Mark, Luke, or John) our bodies are at prayer, too. We trace a sign of the cross on our forehead, lips, and heart. In this way, we ask that God's Word be in our thoughts and in the words we speak, and that it takes root in our hearts, moving us to praise and bless the Lord and to do good in the world.

The homily that follows is to help us understand what God's Word means and reminds us that we are not alone. God's Word is within us, guiding us, and leading us to worship. The whole assembly then prays the Creed, stating aloud what we believe as members of the Church. In the Universal Prayer we pray for the needs of all God's people.

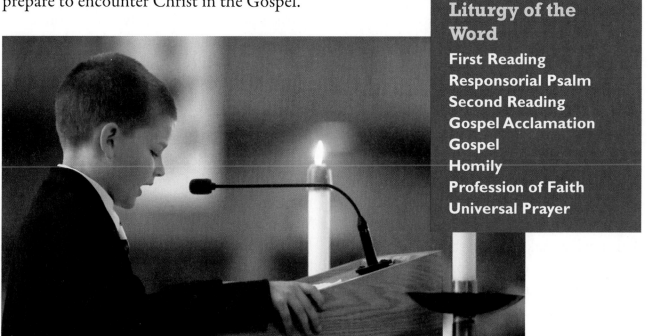

### Liturgy of the Word

**First Reading**
**Responsorial Psalm**
**Second Reading**
**Gospel Acclamation**
**Gospel**
**Homily**
**Profession of Faith**
**Universal Prayer**

## Liturgy of the Eucharist

At the heart of the entire liturgical celebration is the Liturgy of the Eucharist. It begins with the Presentation of the Gifts of bread and wine, and the Prayer over the Offerings. This is a symbolic expression of joining ourselves with the sacrifice of Christ. We should offer not only what is positive in our lives but also our struggles and sorrows. In essence, we unite our whole selves—everything we are and hope to be—with the sacrifice of Christ.

Now is the time for the high point of the entire celebration—the Eucharistic Prayer. We are on our knees, in quiet reverence. The priest, in our name, thanks God for all his works of salvation. Our resounding response of praise is: "Holy, Holy, Holy Lord God of hosts. / Heaven and earth are full of your glory."

We have come to the very heart of the Mass—the changing of the bread and wine into the Body and Blood of Christ. What a beautiful mystery of faith. Jesus is our high priest, and Jesus is present on the altar under the appearances of bread and wine. This is what makes the celebration of Mass the "perfect" act of worship. Jesus is offering the sacrifice through the ministry of the priest *and* is the one being offered. Listen.

You can hear Jesus' words, as the Apostles' heard so long ago: "THIS IS MY BODY, WHICH WILL BE GIVEN UP FOR YOU . . . THIS IS THE CHALICE OF MY BLOOD . . . WHICH WILL BE POURED OUT FOR YOU AND FOR MANY FOR THE FORGIVENESS OF SINS." By the power of the Holy Spirit, our gifts of bread and wine have become the very Body and Blood of the Risen Christ.

Jesus is truly present, even though the appearances of bread and wine remain. We prepare to receive Christ so that he may work in us. Together we pray the Lord's Prayer that Jesus taught us, and we pray that Christ's peace be with us always. We offer one another a sign of peace to show that we are united in Christ.

With your family, watch as the priest breaks the consecrated bread, the Body of Christ. Jesus also made this gesture—the Breaking of the Bread—at the Last Supper. It shows our unity, for in Holy Communion we share in the One Bread that is broken for us all. When we receive Holy Communion with faith and love, Christ can help us to become better, to become more patient and forgiving, and to show greater love and compassion to other people.

## We Go in Peace . . .

In the Concluding Rites, the priest offers a final prayer and blesses us in the name of the Father, the Son, and the Holy Spirit. We hear these or other words of dismissal: "Go in peace, glorifying the Lord by your life." The Mass doesn't really end; it is meant to continue in our daily lives.

How will you and your family bring Christ to the world?

**Concluding Rites**
Greeting
Blessing
Dismissal

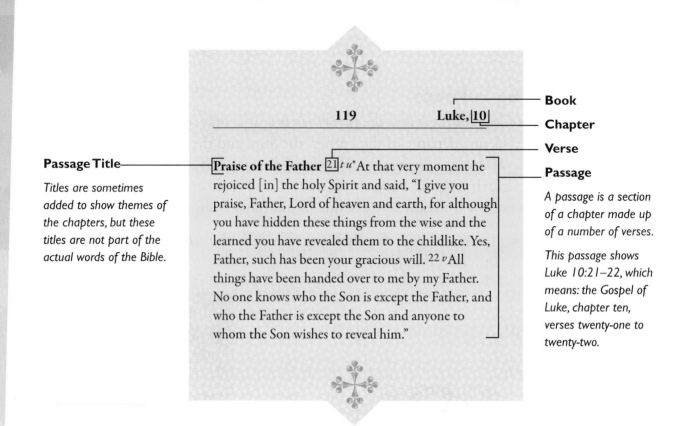

**Book**

**Chapter**

**Verse**

**Passage**

**Passage Title**

Titles are sometimes added to show themes of the chapters, but these titles are not part of the actual words of the Bible.

**Praise of the Father** 21 *t u** At that very moment he rejoiced [in] the holy Spirit and said, "I give you praise, Father, Lord of heaven and earth, for although you have hidden these things from the wise and the learned you have revealed them to the childlike. Yes, Father, such has been your gracious will. 22 *v* All things have been handed over to me by my Father. No one knows who the Son is except the Father, and who the Father is except the Son and anyone to whom the Son wishes to reveal him."

A passage is a section of a chapter made up of a number of verses.

This passage shows Luke 10:21–22, which means: the Gospel of Luke, chapter ten, verses twenty-one to twenty-two.

## Reading the Bible . . . in Five Easy Steps

When you are given a Scripture passage to read, here are five easy steps that will help you to find it! With your child, follow these steps to look up **Lk 10:21–22.**

1. **Find the book.** When the name of the book is abbreviated, locate the meaning of the abbreviation on the contents pages at the beginning of your Bible. *Lk* stands for Luke, one of the four Gospels.

2. **Find the page.** Your Bible's contents pages will also show the page on which the book begins. Turn to that page within your Bible.

3. **Find the chapter.** Once you arrive at the page where the book begins, keep turning the pages forward until you find the right chapter. The image above shows you how a chapter number is usually displayed on a typical Bible page. You are looking for chapter **10** in Luke.

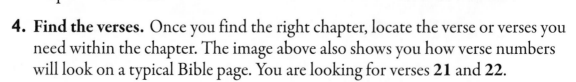

4. **Find the verses.** Once you find the right chapter, locate the verse or verses you need within the chapter. The image above also shows you how verse numbers will look on a typical Bible page. You are looking for verses **21** and **22.**

5. **Start reading!**

## Stations of the Cross

In the Stations of the Cross, we follow in the footsteps of Jesus during his Passion and Death on the Cross.

1. Jesus is condemned to die.
2. Jesus takes up his Cross.
3. Jesus falls the first time.
4. Jesus meets his mother.
5. Simon helps Jesus carry his Cross.
6. Veronica wipes the face of Jesus.
7. Jesus falls the second time.

8. Jesus meets the women of Jerusalem.
9. Jesus falls the third time.
10. Jesus is stripped of his garments.
11. Jesus is nailed to the Cross.
12. Jesus dies on the Cross.
13. Jesus is taken down from the Cross.
14. Jesus is laid in the tomb.

## Celebrating Penance and Reconciliation

How do we show God we are sorry? When we receive the Sacrament of Penance and Reconciliation, we show we are sorry for our sins by confessing them to the priest and doing the penance we receive. Another name for showing we are sorry is repentance. Review the steps to receive the Sacrament of Penance below. Make a commitment as a family to receive the Sacrament of Penance at least once a year.

### Steps to Receive the Sacrament of Penance

- The priest welcomes me, and we both make the Sign of the Cross.

- Sometimes the priest reads a story from the Bible about God's forgiveness.

- I confess my sins to the priest.

- The priest may talk to me about what I can do to make the right choices. He will give me a penance to do. A penance is a prayer or action that shows I am sorry for my sins. I will carry out my penance after the celebration of the sacrament.

- I pray the Act of Contrition, expressing my sorrow for my sins and my intention to avoid sin in the future.

- I receive absolution, or forgiveness, from my sins.

- I join the priest in giving thanks for God's forgiveness.

## Examination of Conscience

Before you go to confession, it is helpful to quietly sit and examine your conscience. Use these questions to help you reflect on your relationship with God and others.

Do I make anyone or anything more important to me than God?

Have I read from the Bible and prayed?

Do I respect God's name and the name of Jesus?

Do I participate in Mass and keep Sunday holy by what I say and do?

Do I show obedience to God by my obedience to parents, guardians, and teachers?

Have I hurt others by my words and actions? Have I helped those in need?

Do I respect myself? Do I take good care of my body and show respect to others? Do I respect the dignity of everyone I meet?

Have I been selfish or taken the belongings of others without their permission? Have I shared my belongings?

Have I been honest? Have I lied or cheated?

Do I speak, act, and dress in ways that show respect for myself and others?

Have I been happy for others when they have the things they want or need?

## The Ten Commandments

1. I am the LORD your God: you shall not have strange gods before me.

2. You shall not take the name of the LORD your God in vain.

3. Remember to keep holy the LORD's Day.

4. Honor your father and your mother.

5. You shall not kill.

6. You shall not commit adultery.

7. You shall not steal.

8. You shall not bear false witness against your neighbor.

9. You shall not covet your neighbor's wife.

10. You shall not covet your neighbor's goods.

## The Great Commandment

"You shall love the Lord, your God, with all your heart, with all your soul, and with all your mind. This is the greatest and the first commandment. The second is like it: You shall love your neighbor as yourself."

Matthew 22:37–39

## The New Commandment

"I give you a new commandment: love one another. As I have loved you, so you also should love one another. This is how all will know that you are my disciples, if you have love for one another."

John 13:34–35

## The Beatitudes

"Blessed are the poor in spirit, for theirs is the kingdom of heaven."

"Blessed are they who mourn, for they will be comforted."

"Blessed are the meek, for they will inherit the land."

"Blessed are they who hunger and thirst for righteousness, for they will be satisfied."

"Blessed are the merciful," for they will be shown mercy."

"Blessed are the clean of heart, for they will see God."

"Blessed are the peacemakers, for they will be called children of God."

"Blessed are they who are persecuted for the sake of righteousness, for theirs in the kingdom of heaven."

Matthew 5:3–10

249

## The Seven Sacraments

### The Sacraments of Christian Initiation
Baptism
Confirmation
Eucharist

### The Sacraments of Healing
Penance and Reconciliation
Anointing of the Sick

### The Sacraments at the Service of Communion
Holy Orders
Matrimony

## The Power of Grace

How do we live as disciples of Jesus? Through the power of God's grace, we can grow in our friendship with God. Grace is a share in God's life and love. We receive grace at our baptism and when we receive the other sacraments. The water of Baptism is a sign of the life that God gives us through his grace. Throughout our lives, grace helps us respond to God with love. It gives us the strength to live as Jesus' disciples.

# Your *Christ In Us*

# Family Companion

**W**elcome. We are so glad that you are a ***Christ In Us*** family. In this section, you will find a treasury of resources as your family accompanies your child on our journey to a greater love in Jesus Christ. This material is written specifically for you as adult family members. But be certain that you review your child's resources that precede this section. Also, don't forget to look over the *Glossary* that follows. It will give you a good overview of what your child has been experiencing this year. Finally, the *Q&A* offers a wonderful opportunity for your entire family to review the major faith statements of the grade.

## Mass, Confession, and Our Catholic Obligation

Is your family aware that as Catholics we are obliged to attend Sunday Mass and to confess our sins at least once a year? These are part of the Precepts of the Church, laws of the Church that help us to see that loving God and others is connected to our life of prayer and worship and to our life of service. They guide our behavior and teach us how we should act as members of the Church. They remind us that we are called to grow in holiness and serve the Church. As a family, familiarize yourselves with the precepts of the Church.

### The Precepts of the Church

**1.** You shall attend Mass on Sundays and holy days of obligation and rest from servile labor.

**2.** You shall confess your sins at least once a year.

**3.** You shall receive the Sacrament of the Eucharist at least during the Easter season.

**4.** You shall observe the days of fasting and abstinence by the Church.

**5.** You shall help to provide for the needs of the Church.

### Holy Days of Obligation

Here are the Holy Days of Obligation that the Church in the United States celebrates:

- **Solemnity of Mary, Mother of God** (January 1)
- **Ascension** (when celebrated on Thursday during the Easter season*)
- **Assumption of Mary** (August 15)
- **All Saints' Day** (November 1)
- **Immaculate Conception** (December 8)
- **Christmas** (December 25)

*Some dioceses celebrate the Ascension on the following Sunday.*

### The Liturgical Year: Moveable Feasts

While some important dates in the Church year are the same from year to year—such as Christmas on December 25 and All Saints' Day on November 1—other dates change from year to year. The Church refers to Ash Wednesday, Easter, Ascension, and Pentecost as "moveable" feasts.

The Council of Nicea in 325 (see *CCC*, 1170) decided that Easter should be celebrated on the first Sunday after the first full moon *after* (but never on) the first day of spring. In the calendars we use today, the first day of spring is March 21. Therefore, Easter can be as early as March 22 and no later than April 25. The date of Easter determines the dates of the other moveable feasts.

Below are the dates of the moveable feasts for the next several years. How does your family celebrate or observe each day?

|  | Ash Wednesday | Palm Sunday | Easter | Ascension | Pentecost |
|---|---|---|---|---|---|
| 2019 | March 6 | April 14 | April 21 | May 30 | June 9 |
| 2020 | February 26 | April 5 | April 12 | May 21 | May 31 |
| 2021 | February 17 | March 28 | April 4 | May 13 | May 23 |
| 2022 | March 2 | April 10 | April 17 | May 26 | June 5 |

## Living a Holy Life

The task of raising a child with a strong moral compass is not an easy one. Our children are continuously tempted to make poor choices. There are so many distractions today that children face including social media, peer pressure, and the devaluation of human life. This makes it difficult for families to raise children who are holy in thought, word, and deed. However, you can help your child build a strong moral character by being a "Church in the home" and creating an environment that places being a disciple of Christ first. It is in the family that we learn to pray and worship God together, to forgive and be forgiven, and to be disciples of Jesus. Think of this as a call to live like the Holy Family: Jesus, Mary, and Joseph. Jesus grew up in a loving, faith-filled home. Jesus was obedient to his parents. Mary, Joseph, and Jesus' family followed Jewish traditions, prayed, and celebrated the religious feasts of their time. Although every family is unique, by creating a home where the family prays together, loves, and respects one another, you will see a shift in the choices your child will make.

Take the time to review with your child what he or she learned about human dignity:

- That we are made in the image of God.

- That God calls us to recognize one another's dignity.

- That we can work toward human dignity by promoting justice and respect.

- That we can be instruments of God's peace.

Remind your child that Jesus treated all people equally and respected the dignity of every person.

Jesus gave us the commandments that help us to follow the way he lived, respecting the dignity of all people. Read and remember these commandments as a family. Let them guide all your relationships—at home, at school, in the parish, and in the community.

# The Seven Themes of Catholic Social Teaching

Discuss with your family how Jesus valued every person. Jesus' life and teaching are the foundations of Catholic social teaching. This teaching calls us to work for justice and peace as Jesus did. As you review these seven themes of Catholic social teaching with your family, ask yourselves: How can we value others as Jesus did?

1.  **Life and Dignity of the Human Person** Human life is sacred because it is a gift from God. Because we are all God's children, we all share the same human dignity. As Christians we respect all people, even those we do not know.

2.  **Call to Family, Community, and Participation** We are all social. We need to be with others to grow. The family is the basic community. In the family we grow and learn the values of our faith. As Christians we live those values in our family and community.

3.  **Rights and Responsibilities of the Human Person** Every person has a fundamental right to life. This includes the things we need to have a decent life: faith and family, work and education, health care and housing. We also have a responsibility to others and to society. We work to make sure the rights of all people are being protected.

4.  **Option for the Poor and Vulnerable** We have a special obligation to help those who are poor and in need. This includes those who cannot protect themselves because of their age or their health.

5.  **Dignity of Work and the Rights of Workers** Our work is a sign of our participation in God's work. People have the right to decent work, just wages, safe working conditions, and to participate in decisions about work.

6.  **Solidarity of the Human Family** Solidarity is a feeling of unity. It binds members of a group together. Each of us is a member of the one human family. The human family includes people of all racial and cultural backgrounds. We all suffer when one part of the human family suffers, whether they live near or far away.

7.  **Care for God's Creation** God created us to be stewards, or caretakers, of his creation. We must care for and respect the environment. We have to protect it for future generations. When we care for creation, we show respect for God the Creator.

## What Is a Novena?

Have you ever prayed a novena? A novena is a devotion of praying for nine consecutive days. The word *novena* comes from a Latin word meaning "nine." *Novenas* have been prayed since the earliest days of the Church. In fact, Mary and the Apostles prayed together for a period of nine days between Jesus' Ascension and his sending of the Holy Spirit on Pentecost (see Acts of the Apostles 1).

Often people pray a novena for a special need or intention. Many novena prayers are in honor of specific saints. Here is one prayer to Mary, the Church's greatest saint, that you might wish to pray with your family for nine days. Ask Mary for her help with your family's needs or intentions.

## Memorare

Remember, most loving Virgin Mary,
never was it heard
that anyone who turned to you for help
was left unaided.
Inspired by this confidence,
though burdened by my sins,
I run to your protection
for you are my mother.
Mother of the Word of God,
do not despise my words of pleading
but be merciful and hear my prayer.
Amen.

## Vocations

When we were baptized, we began our new life as Christians. Our parents and godparents wanted to share their Catholic faith with us. As we grow older, we want to grow in our Christian life as Jesus Christ teaches. Through the Church, God invites us to choose many ways of helping others. This call from God to live our Christian life more fully is our *vocation*.

God wants all Catholics to help others as members of their parish community. Although our vocation may be to serve as a priest or a religious sister or brother, there are other important ways we can serve our Christian community. As a lay person, we can serve as teacher, missionary, or liturgical minister. Prayer and our experience in our parish community helps us to understand God's plan for us.

It is important to understand that we do not have to be a priest or a consecrated person to promote vocations. As parents, we have found our particular vocations. We can help others find theirs, including our own children. It is important to help young people ask God what his plan is for their life.

Promoting vocations is something we can do in our family's everyday life.

## Prayer for Vocations

Dear God,
you have a great and loving plan
for our world and for me.
I wish to share in that plan fully,
faithfully, and joyfully.
Help me to understand what it is
you wish me to do with my life.

- Will I be called to the priesthood or religious life?

- Will I be called to live a married life?

- Will I be called to live a single life?

Help me to be attentive to the signs
that you give me about preparing
for the future.

And once I have heard and understood your call,
give me the strength and the grace to follow it
with generosity and love. Amen.

## Ways to Promote Vocations

- Answer your children's questions about priesthood or religious life; never discourage them or ridicule them if they bring it up.

- Encourage your children to be involved in the liturgical life of the parish as altar servers, lectors, musicians, and so on.

- Have a priest come and bless your home. Have your younger children make a cross to hang in each bedroom in your home.

- Keep an eye open for TV shows and movies that present Gospel-centered role models. Watch them with your children and engage in a discussion.

- Use books and videos to familiarize your children with saints who are priests or vowed religious. Use these lives of the saints as springboards for discussion on these lifestyles.

- Name the gifts of each family member on his or her birthday. Express gratitude for these gifts.

- On the date of your child's baptism, talk about the life of the saint for whom the child is named (or the saint's day it is).

- Discuss your own vocation to family life, explaining that God calls some people to priesthood or religious life, some to marriage, and some to life as single lay people. Talk positively and enthusiastically about the priests, sisters, brothers, and deacons in your parish.

- Tell your children why you chose your particular profession. Who helped you form your decision?

- Witness to your own vocation by telling stories about your own relationship. Let your children see the love and care that parents have for each other.

# Glossary

**Anointing of the Sick** (page 90) the sacrament by which God's grace and comfort are given to those who are seriously ill or suffering

**Baptism** (page 79) the sacrament that first joins us to Christ and his Church

**Beatitudes** (page 112) the teachings of Jesus that describe the way to live as his disciples

**candidate** (page 81) a person preparing to receive the Sacrament of Confirmation

**chrism** (page 79) holy oil, blessed by a bishop, that is used as a sign of the Holy Spirit

**Christian spirituality** (page 170) finding God through prayer, Sacred Scripture, and Sacred Tradition

**common good** (page 116) what is achieved when all people have an equal chance to fulfill their gifts and their unique calling by God

**Confirmation** (page 80) the sacrament in which we receive the Gift of the Holy Spirit in a special way

**conscience** (page 114) the ability to know the difference between right and wrong, good and evil

**contemplation** (page 166) a form of prayer in which we focus our minds and hearts on God's goodness and love

**conversion** (pages 87, 140) the action of turning to God with our whole heart

**covet** (page 123) to wrongly desire something that belongs to someone else

**devotions** (page 74) the many traditions, outside of the liturgy, that help us pray and grow in faith

**Divine Revelation** (page 20) the ways God makes himself known to us

**domestic church** (page 98) the church in the home, which every Christian family is called to be

**Eucharist** (page 82) the sacrament in which we receive the Body and Blood of Christ at Mass

**free will** (page 107) the freedom to decide when and how to act

**gifts of the Holy Spirit** (page 115) the seven gifts that help us follow God's law and live as Jesus did

**grace** (page 38) the gift of God's life in us, which helps us live in God's goodness and holiness

**hallowed** (page 180) holy or sacred

**Holy Orders** (page 95) the sacrament in which baptized men are ordained to serve the Church as deacons, priests, and bishops

**human dignity** (page 105) the natural value and worth each person has as a result of being created in God's image

**human rights** (page 105) the basic rights that all people have

257

**humble** (page 155) being honest about our talents and abilities and remembering that God gives everyone gifts

**Immaculate Conception** (page 44) the teaching that, from conception, Mary was free from Original Sin

**justice** (page 116) respecting the rights of others and giving them what is rightfully theirs

**laity** (page 53) all baptized members of the Church who are called to share the Good News and are not ordained in Holy Orders

**Last Judgment** (page 48) the event at the end of time when Jesus Christ will come again in glory to judge all people

**liturgical year** (page 72) the celebration throughout the year of the mysteries of Jesus' birth, life, Death, Resurrection, and Ascension

**Liturgy of the Eucharist** (page 63) the part of the Mass in which the Death and Resurrection of Christ are made present again through the Body and Blood of Christ, which we receive in Holy Communion

**Liturgy of the Word** (page 63) the part of the Mass where we listen and respond to God's Word

**Lord's Prayer** (page 178) the prayer Jesus taught that has been called a summary of the whole Gospel

**Matrimony** (page 96) the sacrament in which a baptized man and a baptized woman become husband and wife is also called marriage

**meditation** (page 165) a way of praying in which we try to understand what God is saying to us and how he wants us to live

**mercy** (page 87) kindness and compassion shown to someone who has offended or hurt us

**Messiah** (page 30) a word that means anointed one, referring to Jesus Christ

**moral law** (page 108) God's wisdom within each person that helps us know what is right and wrong

**mortal sin** (pages 88) a very serious sin that severs a person's relationship with God

**Our Father** (page 178) another name for the Lord's Prayer

**Penance and Reconciliation** (page 82) the sacrament in which God is with us, forgiving our sins

**prayer** (page 146) talking and listening to God and our response to his will for our lives

**Precepts of the Church** (page 124) our responsibilities as members of the Body of Christ

**reason** (page 108) the ability to think, understand, and make judgments

**religious life** (page 53) a state of life recognized by the church in which men or women take vows of poverty, chastity, and obedience and live in community to serve God and the Church

**repentance** (page 87) being sorry for our sins and trying not to sin again

**Resurrection** (page 46) the mystery of Jesus being raised from the dead and to new life

**reverence** (page 121) honor, love, and respect

**Sacred Scripture** (page 21) the word of God, also called the Bible

**Sacred Tradition** (page 24) the ways in which the Church shares Christ's teachings and applies them to our lives

**sacramentals** (page 66) blessings, actions, and objects that help us live and act on God's grace in the sacraments

**salvation** (page 137) the forgiveness of sins and the restoring of our relationship with God, accomplished through Jesus' suffering, Death, and Resurrection

**sanctifying grace** (page 139) the gift of sharing in God's life that we receive in the sacraments; this grace both heals us and strengthens us to live a life of holiness

**temptation** (page 129) an attraction to sin

**Theological Virtues** (page 115) God's gifts of faith, hope, and charity

**venial sin** (page 130) a sin that hurts a person's relationship with God and can lead to serious sin

# Q&A

**Q:** **What is a covenant?**

**A:** A covenant is a special, solemn promise from God. God promised to love and care for everything he has made—including all of us—forever. *CCC, 71*

**Q:** **What is the Gospel?**

**A:** The Gospel is the Good News that we are saved by Jesus Christ, the Son of God. In the Bible, the Gospels tell us about Jesus and his words and deeds. *CCC, 73, 139, 561*

**Q:** **What is Sacred Tradition?**

**A:** Sacred Tradition is God's truth found in the teaching, life, and worship of the Church. Tradition includes creeds, or statements of our Christian beliefs, along with the interpretation of Scripture. Tradition includes teachings and practices handed down by Jesus and the Apostles. *CCC, 96, 97, 98*

**Q:** **What is the Blessed Trinity?**

**A:** The Blessed Trinity is one God in three distinct Persons: Father, Son, and Holy Spirit. This is the central mystery of our faith and our life as Christians. *CCC, 261, 267*

**Q:** **What is Original Sin?**

**A:** Original Sin is the first sin committed by Adam and Eve. It is not something that we have done, but it is passed down to all human beings. *CCC, 416, 417, 418*

**Q:** **Who is the Immaculate Conception?**

**A:** From the moment of her conception in her mother's womb, Mary was free from Original Sin and its effects. Mary was not weakened by sin and chose not to commit sin all through her life. *CCC, 490–493*

**Q:** **What is the laity?**

**A:** The laity are baptized members of the Church who share in the Church's mission to bring the Good News to the world. They are also known as laypeople or the Christian faithful. *CCC, 246*

*CCC = Catechism of the Catholic Church*

**Q:** **What is the liturgical year?**

**A:** The liturgical year includes all of the important celebrations of the liturgy that are marked throughout the Church year. *CCC, 1187*

**Q:** **What are sacraments?**

**A:** Jesus has given us seven sacred signs of his grace and love which we call sacraments. Sacraments give God's grace to us. *CCC, 1131*

**Q:** **What are sacramentals?**

**A:** Sacramentals are blessings, actions, and objects that help us share in God's grace in the sacraments. They can be objects like statues, medals, rosaries, holy candles, or crucifixes. They can also be blessings of people, places, and food. *CCC, 1677*

**Q:** **What is the Liturgy of the Word?**

**A:** During the Liturgy of the Word, we listen to what God is saying to us in the Scripture readings. The Holy Spirit prepares our hearts to hear and understand how Christ lives and acts in us right now. *CCC, 1190*

**Q:** **What are devotions?**

**A:** Devotions are the many traditions, outside of the liturgy, that help us pray and grow in our faith. They include prayers such as the Rosary or the Stations of the Cross. *CCC, 1679*

**Q:** **What are the Sacraments of Christian Initiation?**

**A:** The Sacraments of Christian Initiation are the Sacraments of Baptism, Confirmation, and Eucharist. These sacraments make us part of the Church. *CCC, 1275*

**Q:** **What is Baptism?**

**A:** This sacrament welcomes us into the Church. We are freed from Original Sin and are joined to Christ and his Church. *CCC, 1277, 1279, 1280*

**Q:** **What is Confirmation?**

**A:** In this sacrament, the Holy Spirit gives us the strength to live as disciples of Jesus. We are sealed with the Gift of the Holy Spirit. *CCC, 1316, 1317, 1318*

**Q:** **What is Eucharist?**

**A:** This sacrament incorporates us into the Body of Christ. We are strengthened by Jesus' Body and Blood, which we receive under the appearances of bread and wine. *CCC, 1407, 1409, 1413, 1414, 1416*

**Q:** **What is the Real Presence?**

**A:** The Real Presence is the truth that Jesus is truly present in the Eucharist. *CCC, 1416*

**Q:** **What is Penance and Reconciliation?**

**A:** Penance and Reconciliation is the Sacrament of Healing in which our sins can be forgiven and we can receive God's grace. We receive absolution, which means we are forgiven through the words and actions of the priest, who acts on Christ's behalf. *CCC, 1486, 1491*

**Q:** **What is Anointing of the Sick?**

**A:** Anointing of the Sick is the Sacrament of Healing by which God's grace and comfort are given to those who are seriously ill or suffering. *CCC, 1527, 1531, 1532*

**Q:** **What is the common priesthood of the faithful?**

**A:** The common priesthood of the faithful means we share in Jesus' priesthood by our actions, words, thoughts and prayers, showing our love for God and our neighbor to the world. *CCC, 1591*

**Q:** **What are the Sacraments at the Service of Communion?**

**A:** The Sacraments at the Service of Communion, Holy Orders and Matrimony, are sacraments that strengthen people to serve God and the Church through a particular calling, such as marriage or ordained ministry. *CCC, 1591*

**Q:** **What is Holy Orders?**

**A:** Holy Orders is the sacrament in which baptized men are ordained to serve the Church as deacons, priests, and bishops. They serve the Church in the name and person of Christ and serve God their whole lives. *CCC, 1593, 1597*

**Q:** **Who are bishops?**

**A:** Bishops are the successors of the Apostles. They are the official teachers, leaders, and governors of the Church. *CCC, 1594, 1595, 1596*

**Q: Who are deacons?**

**A:** Deacons are baptized men who are ordained by bishops for service in the Church. *CCC, 1570, 1571*

**Q: What is Matrimony?**

**A:** Matrimony is the sacrament in which a baptized man and a baptized woman become husband and wife and promise to be faithful to each other for the rest of their lives. Matrimony is also called marriage. *CCC, 1658, 1660, 1661*

**Q: What is Human Dignity?**

**A:** Human Dignity is the natural value and worth each person has because we are created in God's image. *CCC, 1928–1933*

**Q: What is natural law?**

**A:** Natural law describes our ability to reason about truth and goodness, right and wrong. *CCC, 1978, 1979*

**Q: What are the Beatitudes?**

**A:** The Beatitudes are Jesus' teachings that describe the way God wants us to live every day. *CCC, 1715, 1726*

**Q: What is moral law?**

**A:** Moral law is established in God's eternal law. It is a universal truth that is unconditional and eternal. *CCC, 1950–1953*

**Q: What is conscience?**

**A:** Our conscience is given to us by God to help us know the difference between right and wrong, between good and evil. *CCC, 1799*

**Q: What are the Theological Virtues?**

**A:** The Theological Virtues are faith, hope, and charity. *CCC, 1812–1827*

**Q: What are the Ten Commandments?**

**A:** The Ten Commandments are God's laws that were given to Moses, to help people know how to love God and others. *CCC, 1980, 1983*

**Q:** **What is reverence?**

**A:** Reverence means honor, love, and respect. *CCC,* 2052–2055

**Q:** **What does it mean to covet?**

**A:** To covet means to wrongly desire something that belongs to someone else. *CCC,* 2055

**Q:** **What are the Precepts of the Church?**

**A:** The Precepts of the Church are rules given to us to help us know our responsibilities as members of the Church. *CCC,* 2047, 2048

**Q:** **What is temptation?**

**A:** Temptation is an attraction to choose sin. When we are tempted to sin, we can look to Jesus as an example of what to do. *CCC,* 2846–2849

**Q:** **What is mortal sin?**

**A:** Mortal sin breaks our friendship with God. Those who commit mortal sin lose sanctifying grace. *CCC,* 1857, 1859, 1861

**Q:** **What is venial sin?**

**A:** Venial sin is a less serious sin that hurts a person's relationship with God. *CCC,* 1874, 1875

**Q:** **What is grace?**

**A:** Grace is a share of God's life within us. We receive the gift of God's grace through the Holy Spirit. *CCC,* 1996, 1997, 2000

**Q:** **What is sanctifying grace?**

**A:** Sanctifying grace is the gift of sharing in God's life that we receive in the sacraments. *CCC,* 2020

**Q:** **What is prayer?**

**A:** Prayer is listening and talking to God. We can pray at any time and in any place. We can pray aloud or in silence. We can pray by ourselves or with others. The celebration of the Mass is the Church's greatest prayer. *CCC,* 2590

**Q:** **What is a petition?**

**A:** To petition means to ask for something. In prayers of petition, we ask God for something, either for ourselves or for others. *CCC,* 2629, 2800

**Q:** **What are the two kinds of silent prayer?**

**A:** In meditation, we seek to understand how God is working in our lives and what he wants for us. In contemplation, we become aware of Christ's loving presence. *CCC, 2707–2708, 2709–2719*

**Q:** **What is the Communion of Saints?**

**A:** The Communion of Saints is the family of the Church. They pray with us and for us. *CCC, 960, 1053, 1054*

**Q:** **What is the season of Advent?**

**A:** Advent is a season of joy and hopeful waiting for the birth of Jesus Christ, our Savior. *CCC, 524*

**Q:** **What is the season of Christmas?**

**A:** Christmas is a celebration of the Incarnation, the Son of God becoming man in the person of Jesus Christ. *CCC, 525, 529*

**Q:** **What is the season of Lent?**

**A:** Lent is a time of conversion. We turn away from sin and turn back to God, the source of all life and goodness. *CCC, 540*

**Q:** **What do we remember during the Triduum?**

**A:** During the Triduum, which lasts three days, we remember the events of Jesus' Passion, Death, and Resurrection. *CCC, 1168*

**Q:** **What do we celebrate at Easter?**

**A:** Easter celebrates the new life of Christ's Resurrection. *CCC, 640, 1076*

**Q:** **What is Pentecost Sunday?**

**A:** Pentecost Sunday, fifty days after Easter, is a celebration of the coming of the Holy Spirit. *CCC, 731, 737*

**Q:** **What is Ordinary Time?**

**A:** Ordinary Time is the longest season in the liturgical calendar. During Ordinary Time, the Church celebrates the life of Jesus Christ. We listen to his teachings and try to act as he did. *CCC, 1163*

# Index